ABOUT THE BOOK

Everyone, no matter how young, remembers a time past when the world seemed at once better and worse. But no one ever remembered more vividly and hauntingly than the poet and storyteller James Still, who in this meaningful book recaptures youth in Depression years in the Kentucky hill country where he has spent most of his life. Though he calls his tale fiction, it's so true to life it could well be fact.

Mr. Still's knowledge of life transcends sociology; he knows that Depression does not mean downtrodden or sad. The narrator of this compelling story has wonderful kinfolk—Pap, Mother, Uncle Jolly, sister Holly, and a bright baby brother so surprised by the world that he doesn't want to speak to it. And there are wonderful friends and enemies—a teacher known as Mama Bear, Tavis, Cleve Harben, the tallest woman earthly, widow Sula Basham, and countless others. All have a common trait: a love of life that enriches their daily experiences.

In adventure after adventure these lively people demonstrate it is the courage and humor you bring to life that really count! It doesn't matter so much that the mine closes, that the family goes hungry, that Uncle Jolly acts silly. What matters is that people survive, love, get angry, laugh, and are ever acutely aware of the beauties and dangers of the places they live. As Mr. Still brilliantly demonstrates, life is also language. And none ever was captured more vividly than that of these hill people, some of whose phrases are explained clearly in footnotes.

The drawings by Janet McCaffery, who has illustrated previous popular books by James Still, enhance the fabulous story of a fabulous people and land.

SPORTY CREEK

a novel about
an Appalachian boyhood

by James Still

illustrated by Janet McCaffery

G. P. Putnam's Sons · New York

Copyright © 1977 by James Still
All rights reserved.
Published simultaneously in Canada by
Longman Canada Limited, Toronto.
Printed in the United States of America
08280

Library of Congress Cataloging in Publication Data
Still, James, 1906–
Sporty Creek.
SUMMARY: When work ceases in the Kentucky coal mines during the Depression, a young boy and his family move to the mountains to live off of their land.
1. Appalachian region—Fiction. 2. Depressions—1929—Fiction.] 3. Family   life—Fiction. I. McCaffery, Janet. II. Title.
PZ7.S8565Sp   [Fic]   76-47538
ISBN 0-399-20577-2
ISBN 0-399-61066-9 lib. bdg.

FOR
MY BROTHERS AND SISTERS:
ALFRED, CARRIE LOIS, COMER, DON,
ELLOREE, INEZ, LONIE, NIXIE, AND TOM

I remember my youth and the feeling
that I could last forever, outlast the sea, the earth and all
men.

— JOSEPH CONRAD

1

simon brawl

I ran into the fields one April morning, thinking to climb to the benchland where Uncle Jolly was breaking new ground. The sky was as blue as a bottle. A rash of green covered the sheltered fence edges, though the beech and poplar trees were still brown and bare. I began to climb, hands on knees, the way being steep. I went up through a redbud thicket swollen with unopened bloom and leaf, coming at last to where Uncle Jolly was plowing. He had already broken a half acre of furrows in the rooty earth.

My family had moved from Houndshell mine camp in time to grub* fields for a corn crop and put in a sass† patch. Although I was born on Sporty Creek, more than half of my life had been spent at mine camps where Pap worked in good years. Bad times at the mines brought us

*grub: remove sprouts by digging
†sass: vegetables

back to Old Place, our home seat a quarter of a mile below Uncle Jolly's farm. Uncle Jolly lived in the head of the hollow. Up Sporty the creek bed was the road.

"Whoa-ho," Uncle Jolly said when he saw me. He drew rein and leaned against the plow handles, blowing. He whistled a long redbird whistle. His forehead was moist, his shirt stuck to his back. He'd been hustling the mule and was glad of the rest. "Hain't you got a sup of water?" he asked. "I'm dryer than a preacher's hat."

"I never thought to bring water," I said. "I've come up to learn to plow."

A drop of sweat hung and stretched on Uncle Jolly's chin.

"Jumping Josie!" he said. "This gentleman would pull you clear over the plow handles."

"Now, no," I said. "I'm a-mind to learn."

I was happy he wasn't plowing Jenny Peg, his anticky* horse. He had taught her many a prank. Uncle Jolly was a trickster. Said Pap, "Keep your eyes skinned in his neighborhood. Anybody with a standing order for hens' teeth, wheelbarrow seed, and 'possum bushes needs watching." On the other hand, our movings were a standing joke to Uncle Jolly. He called Pap "the last of the mountain gypsies." Pap countered with Uncle Jolly's courting troubles. Uncle Jolly was thirty and had never found a wife.

Uncle Jolly grinned, scratching into the thick of his hair. "A tadwhacker† never caught on too young," he said. "Just you fetch me a jug of spring water, and then I'll let you try a furrow or two."

He hung the reins about his neck and leveled the plow.

---

*anticky: clownish
†tadwhacker: boy

He dug a shoe toe into the black dirt. "I'm a stump-chewing nag if this ground won't make corn. It's as black as Old Scratch's* heart and as rich as sin."

I footed downhill and back, bringing the water. Uncle Jolly stuck a finger into the jug's ear, swinging it to his shoulder. He drank loud, gulping swallows. Water ran down his neck. It drained under his collar. Not till then did he poke his tongue out, tasting. "Seems to me a family of frogs have been washing their warts in the spring," he said. "Hit's got a powerful whang."† He took another long drink. He must have downed a quart. "I like a wild taste," he said. "The wilder, the better."

"What's the mule's name?" I asked.

Uncle Jolly sat the jug down. "Banged if I know," he said. "If I've asked the gentleman once, I've asked him a jillion times. He won't tell me. My opinion, he ought to be called Simon Brawl, he's so feisty. To start him going, I have to take measures. No trouble to stop him, though. He's a mule. What he wants is to stay stopped."

A flock of flax-birds circled the newground, their cries sowing the air. *Per-chic-o-ree, per-chic-o-ree.* They settled at the field's edge, and it was as if the dry stickweeds had burst yellow blossoms. They pecked at seed heads. They rattled the dry pods of milkweed.

Uncle Jolly studied the plowed area of the field. His furrows were straight as a measure, running true without a bobble. "Hain't many folks know how to tend dirt," he said. "A mighty piddling few. Land a-wasting and washing. Up and down Sporty, it's the same. Timber cut off and rain eating the hills away. Alike, hit is, on Ballard Creek, Cain Branch, Sugar Orchard, and Deer Lick.

---

*Old Scratch: devil
†whang: taste and smell

What's folks going to live on when these hills wear to a nub?"

"I aim to learn proper," I said.

He lifted the plow, setting the point into the ground. I stood there, not knowing what to do. "Best you walk betwixt the handles to get the hang of it," he said. I stepped between, holding to the crosspiece. Uncle Jolly grasped the handle ends and clucked. The mule didn't move. He whistled and shouted, but he might as well have been talking to a tree.

Grinning, Uncle Jolly said, "See what I mean? This fool beast won't stir. He's too trifling even to be called a mule, low as that is. His brains are in his heels." He tried a string of names: "Git along, Jack! Pete! Crowbar! Leadfoot!" When nothing availed, he reached down and caught up a handful of dirt and threw it onto the mule's back. The mule started to move, shivers quivering his flanks. "It's like that every time I halt," Uncle Jolly said. "A mule has a nature plime-blank* the same as a man. Stubborn as crabgrass."

The earth parted. It fell back from the shovel plow. It boiled over the share. I walked the fresh furrow, and dirt welled between my toes. There was a smell of mosses, of bruised sassafras roots, of sweet anise. We broke out three furrows. Then Uncle Jolly stood aside and let me hold the handles. The mule noted the change but kept going. The share rustled like drifted leaves. It spoke up through the handles. I felt the earth flowing, steady as time.

I turned the plow at the end of the third row. "This land is so rooty," Uncle Jolly said, "I'm going to let you work over what I've already broken. You can try busting

---

*plime-blank: exactly

the balks.* Strike center, and go straight as a die."

I grasped the reins and handles. "Get along," I called, big as life. The mule didn't budge. Neither did he lift an ear.

"He's a regular Simon Brawl all right," Uncle Jolly said.

The mule started after I threw dirt on him. He traveled the first row peart† enough, ears standing ends up, for Uncle Jolly began singing at the top of his voice:

> O, I had a little gray mule,
> His name was Simon Brawl,
> He could kick a chew tobacco
>   Out of yore mouth
> And never touch your jawl.**

I plowed three furrows, and pride swelled in me as sap expands a willow bud. I was being master where till now I'd only stood in awe. I was finding strength I'd no knowing of. When I doubled back again, I saw Uncle Jolly sitting on the ground, leaning against a chestnut stump, eyes closed to the sun. The mule saw Uncle Jolly, too, and his ears drooped. He began to walk faster. The harness rattled on his bony frame. The furrow wandered a bit, and I got uneasy. "Hold back there!" I shouted, but he didn't mend his pace.

At the fourth row's end I looked anxiously at Uncle Jolly, hoping he would take over. One glance, and I saw he had gone to sleep. I was ashamed to cry out. The mule hastened the furrow, the plow jiggling, scooping dirt,

---

*balk: space between field rows
†peart: smartly
**jawl: jaw

running crooked as a black snake's track. I jerked the lines. I shouted all the mule names I'd ever heard. The share hooked a root, and the reins pulled from my hands. Grabbing up the lines, I called Uncle Jolly, being at last more frightened than ashamed. Uncle Jolly slept on.

We no longer bore north and south. The mule cut northwest, southeast, back and forth, catty-cornered. My feet flew over the ground. We plowed a big *S*. We made a long *T* and crossed it on the way back. I reckon we made all the letters of the alphabet. We struck into the unbroken tract, gouging a great furrow, around and around, curling inward, tight as a watch spring.

I couldn't shout or raise a sound. There was no breath left in me.

A voice sprang across the bench. "Hold thar, Bully!" The mule stopped in his tracks, and I went spinning over the plow. I got up, unhurt. A bellow came from the chestnut stump. It was a laugh almost too great for a throat to utter.

I looked in time to see Uncle Jolly rise to his feet, then crumple to the ground. He threshed about, his arms beating the air, laughing in agony. He jerked. He whooped and hollered. He got up twice, falling back slack-jointed and weak. A fresh squall of joy flowed out of him each time.

And when Uncle Jolly had his laugh out, he came across the field. The mule watched him come, lowering his head, acting a grain* nervous. Uncle Jolly sniggered when he reached us, and I saw fresh laughter boiling inside him, ready to burst. The mule raised his head suddenly. He licked his yellow tongue squarely across Uncle Jolly's mouth.

"I bet that's a wild enough taste," I said scornfully.

------

*grain: bit

2

school butter

"If Sporty Creek ever reared a witty,"* Pap used to tell us, "your Uncle Jolly Middleton is the scamp. Always pranking and teasing. Forever traveling the road on a fool horse, hunting mischief. Heading toward middle age and not wed. Why, he would pull a trick even if it cost him his ears, and nobody on earth can stop him laughing. Laughs like a man dying with the cornbread consumption."†

Uncle Jolly didn't actually need to work. He could pick money out of the air. He could fetch down anything he wanted by just reaching. And he would whoop and holler. Folk claimed he could rook** the horns off the devil and go free. Yet he didn't get by the day he yelled "school butter" at the Sporty Creek school. Why that was such a bad thing to yell nobody remembers. But it had been so almost forever. A person might as well hang red on a bull's horns as speak that taunt passing a Baldridge County schoolhouse.

---

*witty: half-wit
†cornbread consumption: a joke disease
**rook: steal

I attended the whole five-month school session, and I was a top scholar.* My sister Holly wasn't a scimption† to me when it came to spelling. Later, but not that year.

I could spell down all in my grade except Mittie Hyden. But Mittie kept her face turned away from me. Mostly I saw the back of her head, the biscuit of her hair.

The free textbooks I learned by heart, quarreling at the torn and missing pages. My old reader left William Tell standing with an apple on his head. Rip Van Winkle never woke. That year Duncil Hargis was the teacher, and I prodded him, "My opinion, if you'll let the county superintendent know, he'll furnish new texts. Pap says Fight Creek and Buffalo Wallow teachers have brought in a horse load for their schools."

A sixth grader said, "These have done all they've come here to do."

"Sporty allus** was the tail," Mittie said. She didn't fear to speak her mind. "Had my way, I'd drop these rags of books into the deepest hole there ever was."

Ard Trent, my bench mate, snorted. He could hoot and get by, for he was so runty he had to sit on a chalk box. He could have mounted to the top of the bell pole and Duncil not said *button*. Being smallest, he was the pick.‡ He was water boy and could go outside at will. Ard wouldn't have cared if the books wore down to a single page apiece.

"New textbooks will be furnished in due season," Duncil said. He believed in using a thing to the last smidgen.§ And maybe the rumor the Sporty school would be

---

*scholar: pupil
†scimption: fraction
**allus: always
‡pick: pet
§smidgen: the least bit

closed in another year had something to do with it.

He set us to work. I was put to studying a dictionary, and I boasted to Ard Trent, "I'll lay my eyes to every word there be. I'll conquer some jawbreakers." But I got stuck in the A's. I slacked off and read "Jack the Giant Killer." Short as it was I had to borrow a couple of readers to splice it together.

The next visit Uncle Jolly made to our house I told of Sporty's book problem. I said, "Duncil's too big a scrimper to swap them in." And I spoke of another grievance. "School reader stories are too bobtailed anyhow to suit my notion. Wish I had a story a thousand miles long."

Uncle Jolly cocked his head in puzzlement. He couldn't understand a boy reading without being driven. He peered at me, trying to figure if I owned my share of brains. He tapped my head and listened. He claimed he couldn't hear any. "Empty as a gourd," he said.

At this Pap keened his eye at Uncle Jolly and spoke an old verse which, according to him, fitted Jolly to a T:

> Sporty Creek, Sporty Creek,
> Born and bred,
> Strong in the arm,
> Woolly in the head.

Uncle Jolly only grinned. He could take a joke as well as dish them out. He could beat Pap at making verses, and he didn't have to rub up mossy ones either. His were fresh from the teeth. At the moment he was busy counting my brother Dan's toes. He counted five on a foot and said, "I'd have wagered a kneecap there were more. With such a pappy as yours there might have been." Dan looked solemn. He was six and believed all he heard.

Trying to outdo Uncle Jolly was Pap's delight. When

he didn't get a rise out of him on account of the verse, Pap asked, "How are you and that switch of a girl on Bee Branch making out?"

"Courting to marry," said Uncle Jolly.

"Tall time," said Pap, and Mother, who let Pap do most of the talking, nodded accord.

Holly, at the age when nothing we said was accounted worth hearing, grunted, "Humph." She was eleven, two years my elder.

"You've been sparking* several moons," Pap reminded, " 'Tis said,

> Those who court too awful slow
> In the end have naught to show."

"I'm allowing her to get used to me. Breaking her in."

Said Pap, "Don't let her learn too much. She'll throw you down, and who could blame her?"

Uncle Jolly laughed. "Right as a rabbit's foot," he said.

Pap had to hush. If a body agreed, there was no argument.

Uncle Jolly set Dan on his feet and drew two corn cobs from a hip pocket. He knew a bushel of tricks but talking two cobs together was the one we most fancied.

Placing the cobs a span apart on the floor, Uncle Jolly spread palms over them. He passed his hands back and forth an inch above the cobs. He smoothed the air and mumbled, "By hokus, by pokus, legi'main†, kick, Tom, spur."

Over and over he breathed the incantation as the cobs

---

*spark: court
†legi'main: (legerdemain) sleight of hand

crept closer and closer. They moved by the littles until they tipped. Then Uncle Jolly glanced up at Pap. "Now, what were you saying about my cha-racter?"

"Cha-racter is something you're not bowed down with," said Pap.

As the saying goes, Pap was talking to hear his head rattle. We owed Uncle Jolly a lot. When we were starved back to Sporty from Houndshell mine camp during the panic,* he saw to it we did not lack corn for bread. He furnished us meat from his smokehouse and loaned us a milk cow.

Mother brought up a matter which was a botherment. Pap intended to move to Houndshell again when the school term ended, and she was certain Uncle Jolly would support her cause. Wherever we lived, when we said the word "home," we meant Old Place. Sporty was where Mother wanted to remain.

We had lived in Houndshell during the bad days. The mine bore the nickname Low Glory owing to an unreliable ceiling, and many applied it to both mine and camp. At Low Glory eleven men had perished under dislodged pot rocks, fourteen in a wink in a general fall,† and two at the tipple.**

I remembered the smoky air of the camp, the rusty groaning of metal at the mine face. Our stay at the camp had been a misery. Mining dwindled from five days to none. Then Low Glory closed, and nobody worked. The shelves of the commissary‡ went bare, and patched breeches and gaunt faces became common. The Red

---

*panic: economic depression
†general fall: collapse of a large area of mine roof
**tipple: coal-screening plant
‡commissary: general store operated by mineowners

Horse* spared many from starvation. Even Sim Brannon, the mine foreman, claimed his monthly sack of free flour. Although there was talk of a peg† on coal, we understood hard times were everywhere. We had hung on until three-quarters of the houses were empty.

Mother complained to Uncle Jolly, "I reckon you've heard Mr. Hard Head figures on moving to Houndshell."

"When your man was born," Uncle Jolly reported, "they struck a match to see was his feet cloven. They scorched a heel and he's been running ever since."

"Who can forget our hardships at the camp?"

Dodging the past, Pap said, "The mines are warm in winter, cool in summer, and there's a pay packet every other Saturday. If you are short of cash, you can charge stuff at the commissary." As he expounded, his confidence grew. "After a sorry season comes the good. Following every dry spell falls a rain."

"Even now," Mother reminded, "Low Glory is working just two days a week. What hope is there of a job?"

Pap predicted, "Times are changing. It's in the air. I can fair smell it."

"They're apt to bury me when I die," declared Uncle Jolly, "but I'll not bury myself alive in a coal mine."

"You've heard it already," said Pap. "They're talking of closing the Sporty school. Next session the children might have to walk to Buffalo Wallow. Three miles going, three back. Too far for Dan in his primer year. And the teacher has the name of being handy with the limber-jim.** Too handy."

---

*Red Horse: Red Cross
†peg: government control of coal production
**limber-jim: switch used in punishment

"I can foot it," I broke in. "I plain can."

Pap said, "The mines are down now, but Sim Brannon will hire me the first job that rears up." Sim and Pap had been cronies.

Uncle Jolly advised, "Stay home and send the young-'uns to the boarding school at the forks of Troublesome. Hindman Settlement, they call it. Why, I was there myself in boyhood, and I liked it a heap." Troublesome Creek was in Knott County, over the ridge from the head of Sporty. Uncle Jolly's land sat astraddle the Knott and Baldridge County line.

"How long did you stay at the Settlement School?" Pap quizzed.

"A spell," said Uncle Jolly.

"How long was that?"

"Until my head was so packed with knowledge I was scared it would split."

"How long?"

Uncle Jolly grinned. "Four days," he said.

Uncle Jolly rode past the Sporty Creek school on an August afternoon when heat-boogers* danced the dry creek bed and willows hung limp along the banks. I sat carving my name on a bench with a knife borrowed from Ard Trent. I knicked and gouged, keeping an eye sharp on Duncil, listening to the primer class blab, "See the fat fox? Can the fox see the dog? Run, fox, run."

A third grader poked his head out of the window, and reported, "Yonder comes Jolly Middleton!" There came Uncle Jolly riding barebones,† his mare wearing a bonnet over her ears and a shawl about her neck. He had Jenny Peg dressed in finery.

---

*heat-boogers: visible heat waves
†barebones: bareback

"Hit's the de'il,"* a little one breathed, and the primer children huddled together.

A cry of glee rose at sight of a horse dressed like people, and scholars would have rushed to the windows had Duncil not swept the air with his pointing stick. Only Mittie Hyden kept calm. She looked on coldly, her chin thrown.

I crowed to Ard, "I'd bet buckeyes he's going to my house."

Ard's small eyes dulled. He was envious. He said, "My opinion, he's going to Bryson's mill to have bread ground."

"Now, no," said I. "He's not packing‡ corn."

"If I had my bow-and-spike,"† Ard breathed, "they'd make the finest bull's-eye there ever was."

Uncle Jolly circled the schoolhouse. He made Jenny Peg prance. He had her trained pretty. Then he halted and got to his feet. He stood on her back and stretched an arm into the air. He reached and pulled down a book. Opening it, he made to read although he didn't know even the letter his mare's track made. Or so Pap claimed.

Duncil tried to teach despite the pranking in the yard. He whistled the pointer, threatening to tap noggins should we leave our seats. He started the primer class again: "See the fat fox? Can the fox see the dog?" But they couldn't hold their eyes on the page. Scholars chuckled and edged toward the windows. Ard grabbed the water bucket and ran to the well.

Mittie said, "We're being made a laughingstock."

We quieted a grain, thinking what Fight Creek and Buffalo Wallow children might say.

---

*de'il: devil
‡pack: carry
†bow-and-spike: bow and arrow

Uncle Jolly put the book into his shirt and spun the horse on her heels. He pinched her withers, and she cranked her neck and flared her lips and nickered. He laughed. He outlaughed his critter. Then he dug heels against her sides and fled upcreek.

"Sporty will be called dog for this," Mittie warned. "It's become the worst school in Baldridge County. Textbooks worn to a frazzle. Teacher won't ask for new ones. Not strange we've drawed a witty."

Duncil's face reddened.

"Uncle Jolly is smart," I defended, "and his mare is as clever as people."

Mittie darted a glance at me.

Hands raised the room over, begging leave to talk. Some scholars spoke unbidden:

"One day my mom passed Jolly Middleton, and he was all *howdy-do* and *how-are-ye.* He tipped his hat, and out flew a bird."

"Biggest fun box ever was, my pap claims," said another.

Rue Thomas began, "Once on a time there was a deputy sheriff who aimed to arrest Jolly Middleton—"

Duncil found his tongue. "I grant you there's one nag in the world with more brains than her master. Now hush."

Ard fetched in a bucket of water. He whispered to me, "Tomorrow I'm bringin my bow-and-spike for sure."

Rue Thomas tried again, "Once the law* undertook to corner Jolly Middleton—"

"Quiet!" Duncil ordered. He lifted his chin, trying to think of a way to sober us. Finally he said, "We'll have a spell of storytelling to finish the day. Accounts of honor

---

*law: sheriff or sheriff's deputy

and valor." He nodded at Mittie. "Young lady, take the floor and lead with the history of the Trojan horse in the days of yore."

Mittie stood and went forward without urging. I listened although I opened the dictionary and pretended to study. She told of the Greeks building a mighty wooden horse, hollow as a barrel and with a door in its belly. She told of the critter getting drawn into Troy-town, and of warriors climbing forth at night and sticking spears through everybody. We listened, still as moss eating rocks.

When school let out, I ran the whole way home. I wanted to implore Pap not to move to Houndshell. Pap sat on the porch, and the rocker of his chair was stopped by a book. Before I could get my breath, he announced, "That scamp of an uncle of yours has been here again. And he has confounded creation by doing a worthy deed. He's talked the superintendent into promising new textbooks for Sporty, and you're to notify Duncil Hargis."

I stared at the book on the floor, too winded to speak.

Pap bent to free the rocker. Raising the volume, he added, "And Jolly says for you to read this one until your head begins to rattle."

I seized the book. A giant strode the cover, drawing ships by ropes, and the title read *Gulliver's Voyage to Lilliput.* I opened the lid, quickly reading, "My father had a small estate in Nottinghamshire; I was the third of five sons. . . ."

I wore the book like a garment. It rested at night under my pillow, and I carried it to school during the day. No longer did I swing from the rafters of the old mill for pastime or climb the mulberry tree in our yard to check on the ripeness of the fruit. I turned stingy. I wouldn't loan my book, declaring, "I'll be the only fellow fixed to tell about Lemuel Gulliver and what he done. I'm bound it will cap any old wooden horse yarn."

Nine days passed before Uncle Jolly returned. By then our textbooks were shedding leaves to match frostbitten maples. Come the slightest draft, pages flew. Scholars bundled their books and tied them with string or weighted them with pencil boxes and rulers. Pless Fowley's child stored her primer in a poke.*

When I reported Uncle Jolly's message to Duncil, he twitted, "Any news that rogue peddles has a sticker in it. Not an earnest bone in his body, in my judgment."

Mittie tossed her head, agreeing. Yet she mumbled, "I wish a whirlywind would come and blow our books to Guinea. Then somebody would be bound to do something."

"The ones on hand will endure a spell longer," Duncil said flatly.

"Fight Creek and Buffalo Wallow are making light of us," said one scholar.

"They're calling Sporty school a rat's nest."

"Naming us the poorhouse."

Duncil's ire raised. He lifted his pointing stick. "Bridle your tongues," he warned, "else you'll taste hickory tea."

A fifth grader asked, unheeding, "If Jolly comes again, what are we aiming to do?" Rue Thomas opened his mouth to tell of a happening but didn't get two words spoken before Duncil's pointer whistled and struck a bench and broke.

Uncle Jolly passed us again on a Tuesday morning with corn for Bryson's mill. He rode feet high and legs crossed, and he came singing "Meet Little Susie on the

---

*poke: sack or paper bag

Mountain Green." A sack petticoat draped Jenny Peg's hindquarters, a bow of ribbon graced her headstall, and her face was powdered white with flour.

Pless Fowley's child moaned, "Hit's the de'il, hit is." She gathered her primer into the poke. Scholars watched, mouths sagged in wonder.

Ard breathed to me, "I'm seeing my pure pick of a bull's-eye."

Uncle Jolly rode into the schoolyard and bowed, and the mare bent a knee and dipped her head. He set Jenny Peg to sidestepping, hoof over hoof, shaking her hips, flapping the skirt. She ended in a spin, whirling like a flying jenny.* Then, pinching her withers, he cried, "Fool stutter!"

The mare nickered, and Uncle Jolly laughed fit to fall. Away they scampered, and while still in view, the critter lost her petticoat.

A scholar sang out, "He yelled school butter!"

"School butter wasn't named," I said.

"The next thing to it."

The upper grades boys leaped to their feet, angry and clamorous, thinking their ears might have deceived them. They would have taken after Uncle Jolly had not Duncil raised a second pointer—a hickory limb as long as a spear.

Duncil brandished the pointer, and the scholars quieted. They settled, knowing Uncle Jolly would return when Bryson had ground his corn. Duncil closed the grammar he held. Until Uncle Jolly went his way, it was useless to try to instruct. Forthwith he inquired, "Which of you is prepared to entertain us with a narrative of ancient days? A tale to discipline our minds."

---

*flying jenny: merry-go-round—log spiked to a stump

Rue Thomas said, "I can speak on a deputy aiming to capture a mischief-maker and what happened. Aye, hit's a good 'un."

"It's not what I've requested," Duncil reminded sharply.

Ard's hand popped up. "Here's a fellow ready with a tale about Old Gulliver and what he done. A back-yonder story." He wagged a thumb at me.

"Come forward," Duncil invited.

I played shy. I let him urge twice, not to seem too eager. Then I strode to the front. I told of Gulliver riding the waters, of the ship wrecking, and of his swimming ashore.

"He took a nap on dry land, and tiny folks no better than a finger came and drove pegs and tied him flat with threads. They fastened him to the ground, limb and hair. A dwarf mounted Gulliver's leg bearing a sword, and he was a soldier, and brave. . . ."

I related the voyage to Lilliput beginning to end, though the scholars barely attended my words and kept staring along the road. Whether Mittie listened I couldn't discover, for she loosened the biscuit of hair on her head and let it cover her face.

"Be-dog," a voice grumbled as I finished, "I'd rather to hear the truth."

"Ought to hear of Jolly Middleton nearly getting jailhoused," Rue Thomas said. " 'A gospel fact."

Duncil groaned. And he checked the clock. There was still time to reckon with. He gave in. "Maybe we can have done with the subject by talking it to death, wearing it out plumb. Say on."

Rue Thomas babbled, "Once Jolly Middleton took a trip to town. Rode by the courthouse and blocking his path was a deputy sheriff ready to arrest him for some roundyboo.* There stood the Law, a warrant in his fist. Think Jolly would turn and flee? Now, no. Not that jasper. Up he trotted into the Law's teeth, and he jabbed his beast in the hip, and low she bent to the balls of her knees. He reached and shook the deputy's hand, and was away and gone ere the Law could bat an eye."

A primer child whimpered, "What air we aiming to do when the De'il comes?"

Then we heard a *clop-clop* of hooves and saw Uncle Jolly approaching. He lay stretched the length of his critter's back, with the poke of meal for a pillow. His feet were bare, and his shoes dangled at the end of the mare's tail.

An ox team couldn't have held us. We rushed to the windows. Even Mittie craned her neck to see, her mouth primped with scorn. Ard snatched the water bucket and ran outside. I thought to myself, *Ard Trent couldn't hit a barn door with an arrow spike.*

The mare drew up in the schoolyard, and Uncle Jolly lay prone a moment. Then he stretched his arms and legs and made to rise. He yawned near wide enough to split. In the midst of the yawn, he gulped unaccountably, his eyes bulged, his tongue hung out. He seemed stricken. He began to twist and toss. He yelled, "Oh!" and "Ouch!" and "Mercy me!" As if in torment he slapped his breeches, his chest, his skull.

The scholars watched, not knowing whether to pity or to jeer.

Uncle Jolly reached inside his shirt and drew out four crawdabbers.† He pulled a frog from one pocket, a gran-

---

*roundyboo: squabble
†crawdabber: crayfish

ny-hatchet† from another. His breeches legs yielded a
terrapin each, his hat a ball of June bugs. He rid himself
of them and breathed a sigh of relief. Then he straddled
Jenny Peg, spoke "Giddy-yap," and started away. Uncle
Jolly gained the road and halted. He looked over his
shoulder and a wry grin caught his mouth as he shouted:

> School butter, chicken flutter,
> Rotten eggs for Duncil's supper.

Boys hopped through the windows before Duncil
could reach for the pointer. Girls and primer children
struck for the doors. Ard came around a corner with a
spike fitted to his bow, and let fly. The spike grazed the
mare's shoulder, and she sank to her knees. Caught un-
awares, Uncle Jolly tumbled to the ground head-
foremost. The poke burst; the meal spilled. Up they
sprang as scholars sped toward them. The mare took
flight across the bottom behind the schoolhouse, Uncle
Jolly at her heels. Duncil Hargis was left waving a pointer in the yard.

I kept pace with the swiftest. I went along for the race,
satisfied we could never overhaul Uncle Jolly, and I traveled empty-handed, having forgotten my book. Uncle
Jolly and his beast outran us, the same way we shook off
the short-legged scholars. On nearing the creek they
parted company, the mare veering along the bank, Uncle
Jolly plunging into the willows. When last we saw him he
was headed toward the knob.

At the creek we searched the dry bed for tracks. We
combed the willows and the canebrake beyond. We

---

†granny-hatchet: lizard

threshed out the undergrowth between the creek and the foot of the knob. We elder scholars climbed to the first bench of the knob and paused to catch our breaths. We stared down upon the schoolhouse roof. We could almost see inside the chimney. From somewhere Duncil's voice lifted, calling, calling. And of a sudden we saw the girls and the young boys hurrying back across the bottom, crying shrilly. I saw Holly among them. Then we saw Uncle Jolly race out of the schoolhouse with papers fluttering from his arms.

We plunged downhill, retracing our steps. We scurried to join the scholars gathering beyond the play yard. There under a tree Uncle Jolly lay snoring, a hat covering his face, bare feet shining. Jenny Peg was nowhere in sight. Ard Trent stood close, but only Mittie Hyden wasn't the least afraid. Mittie walked a ring around him, scoffing, "He's not asleep. Hit's pure put-on."

The bunch crept closer.

A little one asked, "What air we aiming to do?"

"We'd duck him in the creek if it wasn't dry," Rue Thomas said.

"It would take a block and tackle to lift him," a scholar said.

"He's too heavy to ride on a rail," another made excuse.

Mittie accused, "I'm of a mind you fellows are scared."

"I hain't afraid," Ard declared, and he moved alongside Uncle Jolly to prove it. "I know a thing we can do. Fix him the same as the Lilliputians done Old Gulliver. Snare him up plug-line."

"Who'll tie the first string?" Rue Thomas posed.

"I will," said Ard. "Fetch me some sticks for pegs, and I'll show you who's game." After they were brought, he pounded them into the ground with a rock beside Uncle Jolly's feet. He cut his bowstring into lengths and staked the toes.

Uncle Jolly snored on.

The scholars grew brave. They dug twine and thread out of pockets. They unwound three stocking balls. They fenced Uncle Jolly with pegs and made fast his legs, arms, neck, wrists, and fingers. Fishing lines crisscrossed his body; pack threads tethered locks of his hair. Even the buttons of his shirt suffered tying. They yoked him like a fly in a spider's web, and still he kept snoring.

When they had him bound, Ard played soldier. He stepped onto Uncle Jolly's thigh and mounted proudly to his chest. He balanced his feet and drew forth his knife and brandished it for a sword.

The hat slid from Uncle Jolly's face. His eyelids opened, and his eyes flew wide at sight of the blade. All of a sudden he bucked. Strings parted, and sticks went flying, and Ard teetered. He bucked again, and Ard upset and fell, and the blade raked Uncle Jolly's nose from saddle to tip.

We stared, not moving, though we heard the mare's hooves rattling and saw Duncil coming pointer in hand.

Pless Fowley's child ran among us, holding an empty poke, crying, "All the books have been dropped into the well. Nary a page is left."

Mittie Hyden looked squarely at me and said, "Jolly Middleton is the best devil there ever was."

Uncle Jolly sat up. His bread-jerker* went up and down. He pinched his scarred nose together, and his face wrinkled with joy. "I can't laugh," he chortled. "Upon my honor, I can't."

---

*bread-jerker: Adam's apple

3
low glory

We moved to Houndshell after school closed in February. We were startled by the altered camp. Three rows of houses were unoccupied with windows shattered and doors unhinged. Seven chimneys stood stark where dwellings had burned. The mineowners were paying scant attention to buildings and tenants. Sim Brannon produced a key to an empty house, and we moved in. Nobody said "scat."

Hardly anybody we knew was left, none of my playfellows. Pulleys and cables at the Low Glory tipple groaned two days a week. The shelves at the commissary were only a third stacked. The gob pile* still smoked, and the cockfights in the Hack continued.

Had there been an opening, Sim Brannon would have taken Pap on, but those with jobs held to them like leeches. Sim often sat on our porch in the evening, legs over the banisters, bemoaning the mess in the world. "If the government would take the peg off coal, the mines could see daylight," he would say. Sim and Pap talked on

---

*gob pile: mine refuse

big subjects: there was never a joke. How we missed Uncle Jolly! Hebron Dunford, "the loudest mouth in the hollow," sometimes expounded on our doorsteps, and there wasn't a knot he couldn't unravel. "Your head ought to be in Frankfort,"* Pap would tell him, a grain sourly.

Pap hunted employment. He ginned† a week at a stave mill on Wolfpen. He put in a month mending county roads, breaking rock with a sledgehammer. With his pay he fetched home fifty pounds of soupbeans and a hundred of Irishmen.** Then he got on at Cass Logan's sawmill for five months.

Plank Town, Cass Logan's camp, was nine miles from Houndshell, and Pap was at home only Saturdays and Sundays. He was away when the baby was born. It was a boy, with a cowlick and two crowns‡ in its hair. Sula Basham, the tallest woman earthly, attended Mother. Mother had helped her in March when her husband died of miner's asthma.§

Footing through the woods to Plank Town and back, Pap looked sharp for herbs. He gathered ginseng○ enough to buy a wheel of cheese. Ginseng sold for thirty-five dollars the pound at Thacker. Setting the great cheese on the table, he said, "Beans and 'taters and this should feed us until things start humming." Pap needed new shoes, but he patched his old ones.

---

*Frankfort: governor's chair
†gin: work as handyman
**Irishmen: white potatoes
‡crown: whorl of hair
§miner's asthma: pneumonoconiosis—caused by inhalation of coal dust
○ginseng: aromatic medicinal plant

By August Pap was back on his honkers† in Houndshell. The mill which furnished rough-cut lumber for the
local market had run out of orders. Although sawmill
labor wasn't plumb to Pap's notion, he reckoned it a whit
above farming. "Nobody ever paid me a cent on Sporty,"
he would say.

Unlike Sporty, where school began in July after crops
were laid by, Houndshell school opened in September.
Dan wept the first day. Holly's eyes were everywhere,
learning everything taught. At a Friday spelling bee she
turned me down for the first time, and everyone else, and
received the headmark.* Mittie Hyden wasn't there to
spur me.

Our teacher was so grumpy she bore the nickname
Mama Bear. She kept our noses in textbooks, and few
dared whisper, much less laugh. She had no picks, and
there was not a storybook in the room, and none spoken
of. And if Duncil Hargis didn't know what made a pig's
tail curl, my opinion she didn't know what made a hen's
comb red. We could twist Duncil around our thumbs,
but not Mama Bear. My schoolmates noticed my shirts
with collars as round as Holly's and my scuffed clodhoppers.‡ Our clothes were made at home, our footgear
bought off pack peddlers. I pinned my collars at the corners, to square them. Nothing could be done about my
shoes.

I got acquainted with Tavis Mott. And Sim Brannon's
son, Commodore. Commodore Brannon attended Pine
Mountain Settlement School in Harlan County, and
when he stayed home a week in June, he told me about

---

†on his honkers: (squatting) doing nothing
*headmark: victory
‡clodhoppers: cheap shoes

books he'd read there. "There's a good one named *Treasure Island* that will knock your eyes out. And *Robinson Crusoe*, I tell you, your feet won't touch earth for a week after you read it. There's another one about a young fellow, *Tom Sawyer*, having a master time with caves and robbers and gold. Best one ever wrote." I stored the titles in my head against the day I could get up with them.

September and October passed, and then it happened as Pap had prophesied.

We were eating supper on a November evening when Sim Brannon came to tell Pap of the boom. "They've taken the peg off of coal," he said. "The government has pulled the price tag. Coal will be selling hand over fist."

The baby stuck a finger into the beans on Pap's plate. Pap didn't scold. Instead he said to the infant, "Baby tad, you've come along in a good year." The baby had no name yet. Mother had given the naming of it to Pap, and he had said, "I'll stir up some John-Henrys in my head and see what jumps out. His cowlick tells me one thing, but the two crowns another."

Mother lifted the coffeepot, shaking the spout clear of grounds. Her mind was on the boom. "Let's hope the prosperity endures," she said.

Holly and Dan and I looked at Pap, wondering what a coal peg was. The baby's face was bright and wise, as if he knew.

Pap thumped the table, marking his words. "I say there's no telling what a ton of coal will sell for. There's a shortage of fuel afar north at the big lakes and in countries across the waters. I figure the price will double or triple." He lifted a hand over the baby's head. "The heavens might be the limit."

Mother set the coffeepot down, for it began to tremble in her hand. She thrust a stick of wood into the stove, though supper was done and the room warm. "Will there be a plenty in the camps?" she asked, uncertain.

Pap laughed, spoon in air. "The Red Horse can ride off somewhere else, where needed. Ay, the best time ever to hit this country is ahead. Why, I'm liable to draw twice the pay I get now." He paused, staring at us. We sat as if under a charm, listening. "We're going to feed these young'uns until they're fat as mud," he went on. "Going to put good clothes on their backs and buy them a few pretties. We'll live like folks were born to live."

The baby made a cluck with its tongue, trying to talk. It squeezed a handful of beans until they popped between its fingers.

"For one thing," Pap said, "I'm going to buy a pair of solid work shoes. These brogans* have worn a half acre of bark off my heels."

The cracked lid of the stove began to wink. Heat grew in the room.

"I want me a store-bought dress," Holly spoke.

"I need a shirt," I said. "A bought shirt with a right collar. And I want a game rooster. One that'll stand on my shoulder and crow. And some shoes."

Pap glanced at me, suddenly irritated.

"Me," Dan began. "I want—" But he could not think what he wanted.

"A game rooster!" Pap exclaimed. "There are too many gamble chickens in this camp already. Why, I'd as soon buy you a pair of dice and a deck of poker cards."

"A pet rooster," I said, the words small and stubborn in my throat. And I thought of one-eyed Tavis Mott, who sometimes played mumbly-peg† with me and who went

---

*brogans: rough work shoes
†mumbly-peg: mumble-the-peg—game played with pocket-knives

to the rooster matches at the Hack. Tavis would tell of the fights, his eye patch shaking, and I would wonder what there was behind the patch.

"No harm, as I see, in a pet chicken," Mother said.

"I want me a banty hen," Dan said.

Pap grinned, his anger melting. He winked at Mother. "We're not going into the fowl business," he declared. "That's sure. I always thought boys wanted a colt to prank with, or a bully calf to hitch to a sled. That's what I craved as a growing youngster." He gave the baby a spoonful of beans.

I did want a colt, but that was beyond wish or hope.

Pap went on, "A while ago I smelled fish on Sim Brannon—fried salt fish he'd eaten for supper. I'm of a mind to buy a whole wooden kit of mackerel. We'll be able."

Mother raised the window an inch, yet it seemed no less hot. She sat down at the foot of the table. The baby strained on Pap's knee, reaching arms toward her. Its lips rounded, quivering to speak. A bird sound came out of its mouth.

"I bet he wants a pretty-piece bought for him," Holly said.

"By thunder," Pap said, "if there was a trinket would teach him to talk, I'd buy it." He balanced the baby in the palm of a hand and held him straight out, showing his strength. Then he keened his eyes at Mother. "You haven't said what you want. All's had their say except you."

Mother stared into her plate. She studied the blossoms printed there. She did not lift her eyes.

"Speak it," said Pap. "My ears are pricked."

"The thing I want has been my longing for quite a while," Mother said at last. Her voice seemed to come from a distance. "When it can be done, I want to move back home, and to stay. We can live under our own roof, on land we hold deed to, beholden to none. Now, did we save half your wages, soon we'd have sufficient for another start—a plow, wagon, and horse. And enough to tide us until a crop can be raised."

To pay the haul bill to the mines, Pap had sold our farm equipment and plow animal.

Dan blabbed, "I want to live where Uncle Jolly is." He frowned at the baby, for he coveted the seat on Pap's knee.

My head was in a boil. I didn't know my own mind. I didn't choose to leave the camp, yet yearned for Sporty Creek. I thought of the aged water mill below our house at the Old Place and of the berries which ripened in our bottom or in our yard: strawberries, hackberries, blackberries, huckleberries, mulberries.

Paying Dan no attention, Pap said, "Half? Why, we're going to start living like town folks. Clothes that fit, food a body can relish." He shucked his coat, for he sat nearest the stove. He wiped sweat beads off his forehead. To Pap, returning to the Old Place was all right at some distant future. Not any year soon.

"I need me a shirt," I said again. "A shirt with a proper collar and some shoes."

"No use being paupers in the midst of plenty," Pap told Mother. "Saving half is too much."

Mother rose from the table and leaned over the stove. She looked inside to see if anything had been left to burn. She tilted the coffeepot, making sure it hadn't boiled dry. Her lips trembled. She picked up the poker, lifted a stove cap, and shook the embers. Drops of water began to fry on the stove. She was crying.

"Be-dogs!" Pap said. "Stop poking that fire! This room is already as hot as a ginger mill."

On a Saturday afternoon Pap brought his two-week pay packet home, the first since the boom. He strode into the kitchen, holding it aloft, unopened. Mother was cooking a skillet of meal mush, and the air was heavy with the good smell. I was in haste to eat and go, having promised Tavis Mott to meet him at the schoolhouse gate.

As Pap rattled the pocket, he said, "Corn in the hopper and meal in the sack."

He let Holly and Dan push fingers against it, feeling the greenbacks inside. He gave it to the baby to play with upon the floor, watching out of the tail of his eye. Mother was uneasy with Pap's carelessness.

"Money, money," Holly spoke, teaching the baby.

He twisted his lips, his tongue stretching. But he could not manage it.

"I'd give every red cent to hear him say a single word," Pap said.

The pay packet was opened: the greenbacks were spread upon the table. We had never seen such bounty. Pap began to figure slowly with fingers and lips. Holly counted swiftly. She could count nearly as fast as Mama Bear.

Pap paused, watching Holly. "This young lady can outcount a checkweighman,"* he declared.

"Sixty-two dollars and thirty cents," Holly announced, and it was correct, for Mother had counted too. And straightaway, Holly said, "I want me a store-bought dress, and I want me a gold locket like Sula Basham's."

Mother blinked. She had never owned a piece of jewelry.

I said, "I'm aiming for a dressy shirt." I had seen an occasional man in the camp wear a shirt with stripes or dots.

---

*checkweighman: miner's agent to assure honest weights

Pap's forehead wrinkled. "These children do need clothes. Clothes they're not ashamed to wear. No use going about like raggle-taggle gypsies with money in hand."

"Socks and stockings I've already knitted," Mother said, "and shirts and dresses I've sewed to do for the winter. They're not made by store patterns, but they'll keep a body covered and warm. I'm determined to do without and live hard to get back to Sporty."

"Oh, I'm willing," Pap resigned, "but a man likes to get his grunt and groan in." He gathered the greenbacks, handing them to Mother. He stacked the three dimes. "When I can't see money, I can save without pain. Once it's in my pocket, I burn to spend."

Mother rolled the bills. She thrust them into an empty draw sack and stowed it in her bosom. "If you agreed," she told Pap, "you could bring the pay packets home unopened. We'd save all we could bear, only open one when needed. I say the boom won't last eternally."

Pap pulled his eyebrows, deciding. "Ay, I'm of a mind to," Pap said finally, "but the children ought to have a few coins to pleasure themselves with. A nickel a week, say."

"I want mine broke into pennies," Dan said.

Holly counted swiftly, speaking in dismay, "It would take a jillion years to save enough for a store dress."

"We'll not lack comfort or pleasure," Mother promised. "Nor will we waste. The children can have the nickel. You can buy a pair of work shoes, not costly boots. And we'll have a kit of salt fish."

"The boots I was set on cost eighteen dollars the pair," said Pap. "I'll make these clodbusters do awhile longer."

Mother stirred butter into the meal mush, and it was done. Holly hurried dishes and spoons to the table.

A buttery steam rose from our plates. We dipped up

spoonfuls of mush. We scraped our dishes, pushing them back for more. Then I slid from the table bench and pulled my cap off its peg.

"Where are you running off to?" Pap asked.

"Going to play with Tavis Mott. He's yonder in the schoolyard."

"I know Tavis," Dan spoke, gulping mush. "He's a boy just got one eyeball."

I sped the Houndshell road. A banjo twanged among the houses. Smokes stirred in chimney pots, rising, threading the chilly air. I reached the schoolhouse, breathing hard, and Tavis Mott was swinging on the gate.

"I'd near given you out," Tavis said, jumping down. His lone blue eye was wide. A patch covered his empty socket.

Tavis was a full head taller than I, and a year older. He drew a wedge of tobacco from a hind pocket, bit a squirrely bite, and offered the cut to me.

I shook my head.

He puckered his lips, speaking around the wad in his jaw. "I'd figured we'd go to the rooster fights. Now you've come too late."

"Was I to go," said I, "my pap would tear up stakes."

Two children raced by, playing tag. A man came walking the road. Tavis spat into a rut. The black patch trembled on his face.

"Before long, fellows will be coming down from the Hack," Tavis said. "We'll hear which roosters whipped."

I studied the eye patch. It was the size of a silver dollar, hanging by a string looped around his head. What lay behind it? Was there a hole square into the skull? Could a body see brains? I was almost ashamed to ask, almost afraid. I drew a circle on the ground with a shoe tie, measuring the words: "I'll go to the rooster fight with you sometime, if you'll let me see your eye pocket."

Tavis blew the tobacco cud across the road. "You'll spy, then won't go."

" 'F'ad die."★

We saw a man walking the path off the ridge, coming toward us from the Hack. He came fast, though he was still too distant to be recognized. We watched him wend the crooked path and be lost among the houses.

"When we go to the cockpit," Tavis said, "I'll let you see under the rag."

"I choose now."

Tavis was firm. "At that time, I will." He hushed a moment, listening for the approaching man. "Before long I'll not be wearing this patch," he said. "I've heard there are glass eyeballs. Five round dollars they cost, and could I grab hold of that much, I'd get Mama Bear to mail me out an order."

"I'm going to save money, come every week," I said. "I've got something in my head to buy."

"Hit reads in a magazine where a fellow can sell garden seed and make a profit. A hundred packages of squash and radish and turnip sold, I'd have me enough," said Tavis.

We saw the man gain the road. He was heading our way, walking a hippety-hop on short legs. Tavis hailed him as he reached the schoolhouse gate, and he stopped. He shed his coat, being warm from the exercise, and he wore a green-dotted shirt.

"Who whipped?" Tavis asked.

The man's face grew sorrowful. He swung his arms emptily, glancing at the sky's promise of weather. There

---

★'F'ad die: If I had to die

was a hint of snow. "Cleve Harben's Red Pyle rim-wrecked my Duckwing," he grumbled. "Cleve brought that bird from West Virginia and he scratches in all the money. I say it hain't fair pitting a foreign cock." His voice hoarsened. "I cherished that rooster." He walked on, and I looked after him, thinking a green-speckled shirt was the choicest garment ever a body could wear.

Winter came before I could go to the Hack. Snow fell late in November and scarcely left the ground for two months. The cockfights were halted until spring. I recollect the living river of wind pouring into the hollow. For folk beyond the camps, it was a lean time, but the Low Glory miners fared well. The three rows of empty houses were reoccupied, and four of the seven which had burned were rebuilt. A doctor set up practice one day a week in a room adjoining the commissary.

I recall the warm coats, the woolen gloves, the high-top boots on men other than Pap. Pap bought the both of us cheap shoes from a pack peddler. I remember the full pokes of victuals going into houses, the smell of ham and sausage frying. Children wore Sunday clothes to school, and Mama Bear wore better to match them. Youngsters bought spin tops and pretties at the commissary. Even boys' pockets clinked money.

Only Tavis Mott and I had to wind our own balls from worn knitted stockings and whittle our tops. I hoarded the nickels Mother gave me, telling Tavis I might buy a shirt when enough had been saved. Tavis never had a penny. He spoke bitterly of it. "My paw wouldn't fetch the turpentine if I was snake bit."

Mother spent little. We hardly dared complain, having more than we had ever known. Once, in January, Pap tried to calculate the amount of money Mother had stored in the draw sack. He marked with a stub of pencil.

"My wages have been upped three times," he said hopefully, "though I can't calculate how much." Pap couldn't much more than count his fingers, although he wouldn't have admitted it.

"I've no idea of the total myself," Mother said. "I opened two pay packets, and we're living out of it. The rest I've kept sealed."

Pap asked, "How's a person to know when enough has been gathered? The men on my shift are beginning to claim the buffalo bellows when I spend a nickel."

"If you want something bad enough, you'll give up for it," Mother said. "You'll sacrifice. The coal famine is bound to end someday. Come that time, it's back to Sporty Creek for us, and in good financial shape."

Pap began to wheedle. "What say we count the greenbacks? Curiosity is eating me raw."

"Now, no. It would be a temptation to spend."

The baby sat up, threshing the air, puckering his lips. We looked, and he had bitten the rubber tip off the pencil.

"Hain't he old enough to say words?"

"What he's old enough for is to have a name," reminded Mother. "Past due."

Pap said, "I'm still thinking on it." He stuck a finger in the baby's mouth and retrieved the rubber tip. He plucked its chin. "By golly, if he'd just speak one word I might name him Noah—Noah Webster."

The baby lifted his arms, mouth wide, neck stretched. He crowed.

"There's your rooster." Pap chuckled, setting his eyes on me.

"I aim to own a real gamer," I said, irked by Pap's teasing. "I aim to."

"This zero weather is a good thing in one particular," Pap drawled. "It has driven the poker players and the chicken gamblers indoors. But they'll be at it again come April. Hit's high-low-jack and the fools lose every button cent."

"I call the boom a gamble," Mother said. "It's bound to be over eventually. We've had them before."

I told Tavis of Mother's prophecy as we sat by a fire on the creek bank. We were fishing through holes in the ice.

"I'm in be-hopes the boom lasts until I git me a glass eye," he said. "My heart is set on it. I'd better have me a batch of garden seeds ordered and start selling."

"You couldn't stick a pickax in the ground it's so froze," I told him. "Folks won't buy seeds in winter."

Tavis rubbed his hands over the blaze. His breath steamed. "Winter hain't going to last forever either," he said.

I recollect thinking the long cold spell might actually be eternal. January dawdled. February crawled. March warmed a bit, and at last the ground thawed.

Tavis got his seeds, though when he should have been peddling them, he would climb the ridge to the Hack. When a rooster was slain, they would often give him the dead fowl. Pap forbade my going along, but next to seeing was Tavis's telling. I came to know the names of the bravest cocks. I knew their markings and the style they fought.

Tavis whistled for me on a Saturday evening at the edge of dark. I heard and went outside. He stood beyond the fence with a flour poke bundled in his arms. He seemed fearful and anxious, yet proud. His lone blue eye was wide. Packets of seeds rattled in his pockets.

"How much money have you saved?" he inquired. "How much?" His voice was a husky whisper.

I guessed what the bundle held, scarcely daring to believe. I grew feverish with wonder.

"Eleven nickels," I said. "I couldn't save all."

The flour sack moved. Something threshed inside. It was a fowl beating its wings.

"I'm of a mind to sell you half ownership in my rooster," he said. "I will for your eleven nickels and if you'll keep him till I find him a hiding place. My pap would wring its neck did I take him home."

I touched the bundle. My hand trembled. "I've been saving to buy me a shirt," I said. "A boughten shirt."

"You couldn't save enough by Kingdom Come.* Fork over your eleven nickels, and we'll go halvers."

I brought my tobacco sack bank and Pap's mine lamp. We stole under my home and penned the rooster in a hen coop. Pap's voice droned above in the kitchen. Tavis lit the lamp to count the money. The rooster stood blinking. red-eyed, alert. His shoulders were white, reddening at the wing bows. Blood beads tipped the hackle feathers. His spurs were trimmed to fit gaffs.† It was Cleve Harben's Red Pyle.

"How'd you come by him?" I questioned.

"He fought Ebo, the black Cuban, and got stumped. He keeled down. There was a slash on his throat, and you'd a-thought him dead. Cleve gave him to me, and before I reached here, he come alive. The cut was just a scratch."

We crawled from beneath the house. Tavis quenched the light. "Don't breathe hit to a soul," he warned. "Cleve would try to git him back, and my pap would throw duck fits. Bring him to the schoolhouse at two o'clock tomorrow."

He moved toward the gate, my nickels in his pocket. I went into the house and sat quietly behind the stove, feel-

---

*Kingdom Come: end of time
†gaff: metal spur

ing lost without my money, though happy about the rooster.

Pap spoke, trotting the baby on a foot. "With warm weather here seems to me the Low Glory operators ought to pare down on production. Yet they've hired four extra miners this week, fellows from away yonder."

"I know a boy from Alabama," Dan said. "I bet hit's yon side the waters."

"It's United States, America," Holly said. Holly knew everything.

"Sim Brannon believes something will bust before long," Pap went on. "A mine boss might know something we don't. Says it's liable to come sudden. I'm in hopes it won't be like the last time."

Pap reached the baby to Mother. "I'm going to bed early." He yawned. "Last night I never got sixty winks of sleep. Every tomcat in the camp was trying to outmiaow each other on the back porch."

"The fish draws cats. You keep buying kits of them."

I waited at the schoolhouse gate, holding the rooster by the shanks. He snuggled against my jacket, pecking at the buttons. He stuck his head up my sleeve to see what was there. After a spell Tavis came, his eye patch trembling and the garden seed in his pocket as noisy as crickets.

"Why didn't you keep him covered?" he asked crossly. "He might be seen."

"He flopped the flour poke off," I said. "Anyhow, he's been discovered already. Crowed this morning before daylight and woke up my pap. If I hadn't cried like gall, he'd of been killed. Now it's your turn to keep."

Tavis bit a chew of tobacco. He spat into the road and looked up and down. "If I took him to my house, he'd be in the skillet by suppertime." He closed his eye to think, and there was only the black patch staring. "Reckon we'll have to sell him," he said presently. "I figure Cleve Harben will buy him back. He's yon side of the commissary, playing draughts.* Are you of a notion?"

The cock lifted his head, poising it left and right. I loosed my hold about his legs and stroked his bright saddle. He sat on my arm.

"This chicken is a pet," I said. "When I took him out of the coop, he jumped square onto my shoulder and crowed. I've taken a liking to him."

"I just lack selling fourteen seed packets getting my eyeball. If Cleve will buy them, I'll let him have my part. I've nowhere to hide a rooster."

"I hain't of a notion to sell."

Tavis tramped the ground where he stood.

"You stay here until I git Cleve," he said. He swung round. "You stay."

He went in haste, and suddenly a great silence fell on the camp. The coal conveyor at the mines had stopped. It was so still I could hear the *per-chic-o-ree* of flax-birds. I held the rooster at arm's length, wishing him free as a bird. I half hoped he would fly away. I perched him on the fence, but he hopped to my shoulder and shook his wattles.

Back along the road came Tavis, Cleve Harben with him. Cleve wore a shirt like striped candy, and never a man wore a finer garment.

Tavis said, "I've sold my half. Now it's you two trading."

Cleve said, "Name your price."

I gathered the fowl in my arms. "I hain't of a mind to sell," I said.

---

*draughts: game of checkers

We turned to stare at miners passing, going home long before the shift's end, cap lamps burning in broad day.

Cleve was anxious. "Why hain't you willing?" he asked. "Name your price."

I dug my toes into the ground, scuffing dirt. "I love my rooster," I said. But I studied Cleve's shirt. It was very beautiful, and it had a right collar.

"If you'll sell," Tavis promised, "I'll let you spy into my eye pocket. Now, while you can look. Before long I'll have a glass eyeball in."

I kicked a lump of slate into the road. "I'll swap my part of the rooster for that striped shirt. It can be cut down to fit."

Cleve unbuttoned the shirt, slipped it off the frame of his shoulders, and handed it to me in a wad. He snatched the rooster and lit out, the miners going the road glaring at his bare back.

Tavis brushed his cap aside and caught the eye patch between forefinger and thumb. I was suddenly afraid, suddenly feeling no desire to see.

The patch was lifted. I looked and reeled back, squeezing the shirt into a ball. I turned and ran with the sight burning in my mind.

I ran all the way home, going in the kitchen door as Pap went, not stopping the cat that stole in between us. Mother sat at the table, a pile of greenbacks before her, the empty pay packets crumpled.

Sighting the money, Pap gasped, "Hell's bangers!" and dropped heavily into a chair. He caught up the baby from the floor and straddled it on a knee. When he could speak above his wonder, he chuffed, "The boom's busted. Everybody has been laid off. Fired. The big hawk's done lit."* But he laughed, and Mother smiled.

---

*big hawk's done lit: it's over

"I've heard already," Mother said. She shuffled the money bills, flicking them under her thumb like a deck of cards. "There's enough here for a plow and wagon and a horse to pull them. Enough for boots, a boughten shirt, a factory dress, and a few pretties. Enough to tide us over until a crop and a garden can be raised."

The baby opened its mouth, curling its lips, pointing a stubby finger. He pointed at the old nanny sniffing the fish kit.

"Cat," it said, big as life.

4
the moving

The mines shut down. The operators pulled out the machinery and dismantled the tipple. Thieves stripped the copper wiring. The iron rails threading the tunnels to the coal face were removed, and all else which could be taken apart or pried loose. The scrap metal was salvaged: rusted piles of spikes, augers, discarded mine car wheels, tangles of cable. Low Glory was picked clean. Even the road into the Houndshell hollow vanished. A spring tide turned it into a gully.

Families with a place to go sledded their plunder to the highway where a truck could reach it. Some went without certainty where they would wind up, Hebron Dunford exhorting them to remain and tough it out, recalling that Low Glory had a history of resurrections. A childless man and wife walked away, leaving their household goods, taking with them only a budget,* and were not seen more.

Among the first to move were some who had endured the panic years in Houndshell. Sim Brannon left, as did

---

*budget: bag of personal belongings

the men who matched game fowls in the Hack, and Tavis Mott and his glass eye. Three unoccupied houses burned. An empty dwelling had its windows shattered the moment of abandonment. The county closed the school, and the schoolhouse burned the next night. The law arrived, pondered, and departed. No longer did the doctor appear on his appointed Thursdays.

Carpenters tore down four houses and stacked the lumber against the day the road might be repaired. Word flew the whole camp was under the crowbar* and thenceforth moving was accounted desertion. An occupied house would not be touched. Several families set forth at night to avoid sullen onlookers and Hebron Dunford's sermon. The operators' watchdog† hung out in the empty commissary and did not show his face save to accept house keys of departers through a grating.

We stayed on for six weeks. Pap played for time on the off chance Cass Logan might beckon him and we could move to Plank Town instead of Sporty. "Someday when I get my ducks in a row," Pap promised, "we'll settle at the Old Place for all hereafter. Ay, not just now." Yet a quick trip by Pap to see Cass proved there was nothing else to do but to turn farmer forthwith.

In my mind's eye I was already swinging the rafters of the water mill on the stream below our house. Many a secret and dark corner the mill had for hiding and imaginings. Built before the Silver War** for grinding wheat, it had fallen into neglect. Nobody raised wheat anymore. The grindrock was in place, but who knew how to sharpen the burrs? A lost skill.

---

*under the crowbar: slated for dismantlement
†watchdog: company agent
**Silver War: American Civil War, 1861–65

Pap bought a wagon and a hillsider† in Thacker, a plow horse and a rig at a stock sale in Letcher County, and a milk cow from Crate Thompson. Crate was a penhooker** who had driven herds past Old Place in other years. Pap purchased the cow naked,‡ and Mother chided him for not also buying a heifer to come fresh when the animal went dry. As for the horse, Pap said there might be a colt coming along some fine pretty day, and it would be mine.

There happened no high-top boots for Pap, no better shoes for me. The pretties were passed over. As Houndshell had gone from ease to poverty within the batting of an eye, my shirt with candy stripes was too loud for the times.

The day came when the wagon was loaded with our plunder,* and there only remained the nailing down of the doors and windows and delivery of the key to the watchdog. Pap had spent two days patching the road out of the hollow, with no offers of help. Only Sula Basham had been told where we were headed. Holly and I would take turns driving the cow, and she was bound to be first. Holly's nature.

Holly started, the cow on a leash, Dan at her heels. The nanny cat followed, of her own free will. Nobody in their senses would move a cat.

Mother and I stood by the wagon while Pap hammered on the windowframes and spat into the keyholes to make the locks turn. He did what he believed was his duty,

---

†hillsider: plow adapted for steep ground
**penhooker: cattle buyer
‡naked cow: without a calf
*plunder: household goods

useless as he knew it to be. The baby nestled in a wad of quilts in the wagon bed. We waited, restless as the harnessed mare, anxious to hasten beyond staring eyes. Idle miners stood in the yard and scowled; boys tramped the black dust before our gate.

The boys kept glancing at the windows, pockets bulging with rocks. I knew them all, although they had not been playfellows. Five sat in the schoolroom with me under Mama Bear. Two I had known from early days in the camp. I looked into their faces and they were as strangers. Rejection swelled in me like a gorge, for only Tood Magoffin, the man with a child's mind, was heavyhearted at my going. One boy leaned and jerked loose the strings of Tood's shoes.

Though women regarded us from their porches, only Sula Basham came to say a good-bye to Mother. She came walking, tall as a butterweed, her gold locket swinging from her neck like a clock weight. She was higher than anybody.

Sula towered over Mother, and the locket dropped like a plumb to the end of its chain. Mother, barely five and a half feet, tilted her head and gazed upon the locket. Never had she owned a grain of gold, neither broach nor ring nor pin. Cutting scornful eyes at the men, Sula declared loudly to Mother, "You're in luck to have a husband not satisfied to rot in Houndshell, a man who'll knuckle to facts."

The men stirred. Hebron Dunford raised his arms, spreading them as might a preacher. "These people are moving to nowhere," he said. "Why make gypsies of a family? I say as long as folks have a roof overhead, let them roost beneath it. Stay put until things rally."

Men grunted in agreement, and the boys lifted their rock-heavy pockets and sidled toward the wagon. The boys placed hands on the wagon wheels. They fingered the mare's harness. They hoisted the lid of the toolbox to see what was in it. Fonzo Asher crawled under the wagon, rear axle to front axle, and I watched out of the tail of my eye, thinking a caper might be pulled.

Father came into the yard with the key, and now the house was shut against our turning back. I looked at the empty hull of our dwelling. I looked at the lost town, and I hungered for it. Pap held up the key. "If somebody would drop this off at the commissary, I'd be obliged."

Tood Magoffin lumbered in Pap's direction, shirttail flagging. His shirt had been snatched free of his breeches. "I'll bring it," Tood cried, both hands reaching. "I will, I will."

"I'm not wanting it brought," Pap said. He wouldn't trust a lackbrain. "You've got it twisted, Tood. I'm wanting it taken."

Although he wasn't offering to accept the key, Hebron Dunford stepped forward. "Stay, or you'll wish to your Maker you had."

Pap replied testily, "I'd rather perish hunting for work than to dry up in a ghost town." He relished the secret that we owned a house seat and were heading for it.

Cephus Dehart nodded toward Sula Basham and said, "I'll deliver the key if you'll take this beanpole widow woman along and locate her a husband. She's worn the black bonnet* long enough."

Laughter rattled about us. Sula whirled, her face lit with anger. "Was I of a mind to marry again," she spat, "I'd choose nobody the nature of you."

Calming Sula, Mother said, "The devil reward them." She was admiring the locket. Mother was peering at the

---

*black bonnet: in mourning

locket, not covetously, but in wonder, and as if she had not seen it before.

"I'll take the key," Sula told Pap. "Nobody else appears anxious to neighbor you. And when you get gone from Houndshell, you'll find it blessed riddance. You'll praise the day."

Mother climbed into the wagon seat. Sula and Mother were now at eye level. "You were a help in my husband's sickness," Sula said. "You were a comfort when he lay in his box. I hain't forgetting. Wish I had a keepsake to give you, showing I'll allus remember."

"I'll keep you in my head," Mother assured.

"Proud to know it."

"Wherever you set down, let me hear. I'll come visit." Sula was keeping our secret.

We were ready to go. "Climb on, son," Pap bade. I swung up from the hind gate to the top of the load. Over the heads of the men I could see the whole of the camp, the gray houses, the smoke cloaking the gob heap. The stripped skeleton of the tipple lifted above us. The pain of leaving welled in me.

Pap clucked his tongue, and the mare started off. She walked clear of her hitchings. Loose trace chains swung free, and the ends of the wagon shafts bounded to the ground.

"Whoa ho!" Pap shouted, jumping down. A burst of merriment sounded behind us. Fonzo Asher had pulled a rusty.* He'd done the unfastening. Pap smiled while adjusting the harness. He didn't mind a foxy trick. He sprang back onto the wagon.

We drove away, the wheels taking the groove of the

---

*rusty: prank

ruts, the load swaying. Then it was I saw the gold locket about Mother's neck, beating her bosom like a heart.

I looked back, seeing the first rocks thrown, hearing our windows shatter. I looked back upon the camp as upon the face of the dead. Only Tood Magoffin was watching us go. He stood holding up his breeches, for someone had cut his belt with a knife. He thrust an arm into the air, crying, "Hello, hello!"

5

the force put*

"Fetch the lamp," Pap said. "I can't see by the light of this blinky lantern."

Saul Hignight's calf had a cob in its throat, and he had brought it to our place on Sporty in the bed of a wagon. He lifted it in his arms, letting it down onto a poke spread upon the ground. It was a heifer, three weeks old, with teat buds barely showing.

I went after the lamp, but Mother feared to let me hold it. She put the baby in the empty wood box and gave him a spool to play with. She lit the lamp and took it outside, standing over the heifer so that the light fell squarely where Pap wanted it.

The heifer breathed heavily. Her mouth gathered a fleece of slobber. She looked at us out of stricken eyes.

"I'd have brought her before dark," Saul Hignight said, "but I never knowed myself till after milking time. I kept hearing something gagging and gaping under the crib. Figured at first it was a pig snuffing."

"Had you got to the calf sooner, the cob wouldn't have

_____

*force put: a necessity

worked down so far," Pap said. He rolled his right sleeve above the elbow. Saul wrenched the calf's mouth open, and Pap stuck his hand inside, up to the wrist. He wriggled his arm, reaching thumb and forefinger into the calf's gullet.

Saul said, "I fished for that cob till my fingers cramped."

We crowded around, looking over Pap's shoulder. Slobber bubbled on Pap's arm. He caught the calf's throat with the left hand and tried to work the cob into the grasp of his right.

"The cob is slick as owl grease," Pap said. "An eel couldn't be slicker or harder to get hold of."

The calf bellowed, a thin stifled bellow through her nose. Her legs threshed, her split hooves spreading. She breathed in agony. Her fearful eyes walled and set.

Saul Hignight glanced suddenly at me. "Here, boy," he called, "help hold the critter." I moved slowly, fumbling. "Help hold!" Dan sprang forward and caught the calf's hind legs, not flinching a mite. Saul glanced back sourly. I turned aside, though not being able go turn my eyes away.

Pap pulled his hand from the calf's throat. "I can't reach the cob, for a fact," he said. "My fist is three times too big. Three times. Maybe a young'un's hand—"

"Here, boy." Saul cranked his head toward me. "Stick your hand down to that cob, and snatch it out."

I shook my head. Saul grunted and spat upon the ground. "The critter'll die while you're diddling," he said, his voice edged with anger. "Try it. I don't want to lose this one. A bully-calf, I wouldn't mind. But a heifer—"

"Me, now," Dan said. He squatted on his knees. He worked his hand into the calf's mouth and into its throat, nearly to the elbow. He grasped the cob and pulled with all his might. It wouldn't budge. The calf fell back upon the poke, gaping for breath. Her belly quaked.

Saul Hignight stood up. "Hain't a grain of use to try anymore," he said. "She's bound to die. Born during the wrong signs of the moon, I figure." He clapped the dirt from his hands and rubbed them on his breeches. "She would of made a fine little cow. Her mother was a three-galloner. Three full gallons a day, not a gill less. She's of good stock."

There seemed nothing more to do. Saul whistled to his mules and turned the wagon around, ready to start. "I can load the critter and drop her off somewhere down the road," he said. "She's as good as dead. The buzzards will be looking for her tomorrow."

"Let her be," Pap said. "I might be able to dislodge that cob yet."

Saul climbed into his wagon. He clucked and jerked the lines. The mules set off into the dark. "She's yours" he called, "skin and hide and tallow."

"Oh, could we save her," Mother anguished, "there would be milk for us when the cow goes dry. Milk for the baby." The lamp trembled in her hand.

"There's one sure way to get to the cob," Pap said. He weighed the chance in his mind. "One way sure as weather, but the calf might bleed to death." Mother and Pap glanced at each other. Their eyes burned. "Bleed or choke," Pap said finally, "what's the difference?"

"Let me try first," Mother said. She handed the lamp to Pap, warning him to hold it steady. She poked a hand into the calf's mouth, pushing the tongue aside, forcing the locked jaws apart. She worked feverishly. But she couldn't dislodge the cob. She had Holly try. Then she nodded to me. I knelt before the calf, looking into the cavern of its mouth, dreading to put my hand in.

"Hit's no use," Pap said. "Fetch the hone rock, a needle, and thread. And wax the thread."

Mother ran for them, knowing just where the hone was stored and where the needle and thread were kept. She came back in a moment, took the lamp, and handed the hone to Pap. She sent Holly into the house to stay with the baby. "He's fretted with being alone," Mother said. "Find something to amuse him."

Holly returned almost as quickly as Mother had. "I gave him a hen-fooler★ to play with," she explained, "and tore a page from the wishbook† for him to rattle. I left him crowing."

Pap drew a barlow knife from his pocket and snapped it open. He spat upon the hone and began to sharpen the blade with a circular motion, swiftly and with precision. The calf was weakening, being hardly able now to suck breath enough for life. Her eyes were glazed. She picked at the air listlessly with her feet.

The calf was turned to its right side, the head lifted back. Mother reached the lamp to me, telling me how to hold it—close and yet away from knocking elbows. "Both hands under the bowl," she said.

She caught the calf's head between her hands while Pap dug fingers into the calf's throat, feeling for the proper spot. He hunted a place free of large veins. "This is a force put," he said.

The blade flashed in the lamplight. It slid under the hide, making a three-inch cut. Mother looked away when the blood gushed. It splattered on her hands, reddening them to the wrists. Holly began to cry, softly and then

---

★hen-fooler: small gourd used as a nest egg
†wish book: mail-order catalog

angrily, begging Pap to stop. "Stand back, and hush," Pap said. "You make a fellow nervous."

The blade worked deeper, deeper. The horror of it ran through my limbs. The lamp teetered in my hands. Water ran from my eyes and dripped from my chin. I couldn't wipe it away for holding the lamp bowl.

Pap opened a space between the muscles of the calf's neck, steering clear of bone and artery. The calf made no sound. Only its hind legs jerked and its hide quivered. Dan held to the legs, watching all that was being done and not turning a hair.

At last Pap laid the knife aside. He eased thumb and forefinger into the opening and jerked. The cob came out, red and drenched. It spun into the dark. The calf fell back weakly, though beginning to breathe again—a long, strangling breathing.

"Needle and thread!" Pap demanded quickly. Mother reached it to him. Pap folded the inner flesh and sewed it together and then stitched the outer cut. And having done all, he looked at Dan and grinned. "Here's a fellow who would make a good doctor," he praised. "A cool helper. Not one to panic. I'm saying he can call the calf his own."

I handed the lamp to Mother so I could wipe away the shameful tears. I didn't want the calf. I'd been promised a colt.

6

locust summer

Mother's puny spell came at the time the seventeen-year locusts* cried *Pharaoh* upon the hills. Branches of oak and hickory and beech perished where eggs of the locusts were laid. Behind our house a mulberry tree was loaded with fruit. But Dan and I feared to swallow a grub and dared not eat them.

"Berries are poisonous during a locust season," Mother had warned us. She understood our hunger. Pap was doing the cooking and we fared rough. The food got better the week Sula Basham came to attend Mother, grew worse when Mother began to mend and Sula returned to Houndshell.

"It's an all-round plague year," Pap told Mother. "Locusts in the trees and polecats in the barn. The polecats I can't sight, but I have a nose. Still, neither are bothering me as much as these young'uns. Look at their elbows and ankles. They forget to wash their faces, to button buttons. Dirty-eared and more. And look at Holly's hair.

---

*seventeen-year locust: periodical cicada

Ay, hit'll be a pleasant day when you're able to take them back under your thumb. They're wearing me out."

"I expect to strengthen when the locusts leave," Mother said. "A few more days of roaring, and they'll hush." She studied Holly, being most concerned about her. "I can't make a child take pride if they're not willing for it. Holly's hair is a brush heap."

"Silly," Holly scoffed. This was the new byword she had picked up in Houndshell. With Mother ill she did what she tom pleased.

"Don't you know any other words except 'humph' and 'silly'?" Pap asked. "The baby is going to get ahead of you. He can say 'cat.'"

Holly tossed her head.

Dan and I looked sourly at the baby nestled in Mother's arms. For it lately we had nothing but frowns. We blamed it for our having to eat Pap's cooking. Often Dan would crawl under the bed to sniffle, and Mother had to coax him out. He had turned green-jealous of the infant because Mother was doing everything for it and nothing for him. Of my striped shirt Mother had made a garment for the baby.

Holly never complained. She fetched milk and crusts to her hidden play place, eating little at the table. So it was Dan and I who stubbed at meals. The bread Pap baked was a jander* of soda. Vegetables cooked were half raw or burned. We quarreled and said spiteful things of the infant.

Above our voices rose the scream of the locusts, *Pharrrr-a-oh! Pha-rrr-a-oh!* The air was sick with their crying.

Pap would blink at Mother as we grumbled. He would clench his jaws, trying not to smile. Keeping a calm face,

---

*jander: jaundice, yellow

he would say, "No sense raising a chub* nobody wants. Wish I could swap it for a set of varmint traps. I'd give the polecats a hard time. Or, could I find a gypsy, I'd give it away. They'd snatch it, and gladly."

"What I want is a colt," I said, hinting that I was hearing nothing of the promised animal. "I allus did want me a colt."

"A while back," Pap would remind, "you craved fancy shirts and fighting roosters."

I wasn't envious of the baby like Dan. It was just that Pap had made me a promise which hadn't been kept. He had claimed there would be a foal.

That summer we saw little of Uncle Jolly. He was sparking on Bee Branch, and when Uncle Jolly went at anything, he went full blast. "Courting to marry," he would declare. The occasions he did visit us he plucked our chins and pranked with the baby. He would count the baby's fingers, toes, and ears and declare it a miracle they came out to the right number, Pap being its pap. He claimed to like its cowlick better than the two crowns. "The cowlick means he'll have git-up-and-git. Like me."

Uncle Jolly would inquire, "Have you named the little gent yet?" and when told no, he would urge, "If you don't hurry, I'll hang a name on him myself." It was clear he favored the babe above us all.

Pap once asked, "What are you fishing for—for me to name him after you?"

"You could do a whole heap worse."

"Not unless I named him Beelzebub."

The morning the herb doctor and his wife came down Sporty Creek I had gone into the bottom to hunt for

---

*chub: cherub—infant

Holly's play place. She had bragged about it, nettling me with her talk. "It's a really hid spot. Something is there that would peel a body's eyes."

I was searching the thicket beyond the barn when the dingle of harness sounded. A wagon rattled the stony creek bed road drawn by the smallest pony I'd ever beheld, and a man and a woman rode the jolt seat. They traveled with mattress and trunk and stove in the wagon bed. The wagon passed the mill and climbed the rise to our house. I ran after. I hoped Holly had not heard it.

But Holly was there before me. Mother came onto the porch, taking her first steps in weeks. She held the baby, squinting in the light. Her face was as pale as candlewax, and she was letting the baby dangle the locket Sula Basham had given her.

The herb doctor jumped to the ground, his hat crimped in a hand. He was oldy and round-jawed, and not a hair grew on the top of his head. He bowed to Mother, brushing the hat against the grass. He spoke above the locusts, "Lady, is there a chance we could bide a couple of nights in your millhouse? My pony needs rest." From the jolt seat his wife gave Mother a chin hello.* Her hair hung in two plaits about her shoulders. She appeared younger than her husband. She gazed at the baby in its bundle of clothes.

Mother sat down on the water bench. She couldn't stay on her feet any longer. "You're welcome to use it," she replied. "A pity it's full of webs and dust. My husband is off plowing; else he would clean out the trash for you."

I couldn't hold my eyes off the pony. It had a tossy mane that was curried and combed. Not a cocklebur in its tail. It looked almost as fair as a colt.

---

*chin hello: nod

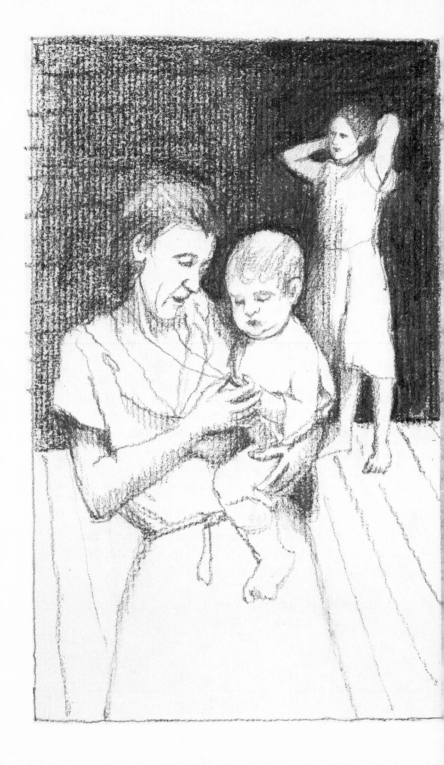

Holly edged closer. She was glowering. "The mill hain't a good place to live," she said.

"We can pay."

"Not a cent we'll take," Mother assured.

Holly became angry. She scowled at the visitors. She doubled fists behind her back. "A big lot of spiders in the mill," she dissuaded. "Spiders with stingers."

The doctor paid Holly no mind. "Lady," he said, "I've seen a lot of sickness in my day." He spread his hands like wings. "When a person needs a tonic to strengthen their nerves, I can tell on sight. Now—"

The herb doctor's wife stopped him. "Doc! Ask about the berries."

"Ah, yes," the doctor said, dropping his hands. "My wife's a fool for mulberry cobbler. Raspberry pie. Berry pies of all descriptions."

"Ask may we gather berries from the mulberry tree," the woman insisted. Her words cracked like broken sticks.

The herb doctor waited.

Mother stirred uneasily. "Wild berries are poison when locusts are swarming," she said. "Always I've heard that—heard it from my childhood. But if you want to risk it, you're welcome."

The herb doctor swept his hat onto his head and climbed up on the wagon. The woman smiled. She was smiling at the baby.

"The mill is a pure varmints' den," Holly declared balefully.

The pony wheeled and set off for the mill. The doctor's wife turned her head and stared at us. She eyed the baby mainly.

That night we children sat at the table with empty plates. Grease sizzled the dove's breast Pap was frying for Mother. "There hain't a finickier set of young'uns in the mountains of Kentucky," Pap groaned. "I boil stuff. I bake, I fry; still, they will hardly taste my cooking. I believe they could live on blue air."

I wrinkled my nose. A musky odor came from the open door. I looked at the bowl of potatoes, at the bud eyes not pared out, at the peelings not scraped off. "I hain't hungry," I said. But I was. My insides felt grown together.

The musk seemed to grow. Dan pinched his nose, and Pap cried, "Whew!" Yet Holly didn't seem to mind. She even grinned.

"There's a polecat rambling," Mother said, covering the baby's face. She fanned the smell away with a hand. "Traps ought to be set under the house."

Pap speared the dove's breast with a fork. "I met a skunk in the barn loft just a while ago." He chuckled. "He heisted his tail, and you can guess what happened to my jacket. It's my pea jacket on the porch that's sweetening the air."

"Hurry the pea jacket out to the woodpile," Mother told me.

I snatched the jacket and ran into the yard. I dropped it onto the chop block. I looked about. The mulberry tree matched the night in darkness. It was as black as its fruit by day. Below, in the bottom, lantern light made shine the cracks in the mill walls. I planned, *Come morning, I'll get a close view of that pony. I'll say to the doctor, "Was Pap of a notion, would you swap to our mare?"* I spat, thinking of our beast.

Pap was talking when I went inside. "I've set traps the mill over, but every day they're sprung, bait gone, and nothing caught. I say it's a puzzlement."

Dan said, "Once I seed a varmint walking. It had a big striped tail. I run, I did."

Holly stuck her chin out, vengeful and knowing. "I told the doctor folks the mill was a den. They wouldn't hear to it."

Mother saddened. "I'd never heard a child of mine talk so brashy to their elders. I was ashamed."

The idea came into my head that Holly's play place might be in the mill or near it. I hankered to go search.

"One thing is for certain." Pap laughed. "Neither young'uns nor varmints will be caught with my bait. I load the table here, and the traps there. What happens? Nothing."

"The children are slipping out of hand," Mother said, her lips trembling. "Holly in particular. Eleven years old and not a sign of womanly pride."

"Holly ought to wear plaits," I spoke. "The herb doctor's wife wears them."

Holly scoffed. "I hain't going to weave my hair into ropes."

"Once I saw a horse go by with a plaited tail," Dan said.

The dove browned and was lifted to a plate. Pap passed it to Mother. The bird was fried hard as a rock. I thought, *I'm so hungry it would take a covey of doves to fill me. I could eat square through the plate.* I felt that empty. I thought of the ripe raspberries in the bottom, I thought of the loaded mulberry tree. I spooned a half-cooked potato from the bowl and tasted. It was briny, for Pap seasoned with a heavy hand. And all of it was the locusts' and the baby's fault.

Pap groaned. "Be-dabs, if the whole family haven't taken the punies. The horse, too. Today she wouldn't eat her corn or hay."

"What ails the mare?" Mother asked.

"She's nearing her condition," Pap said mysteriously.

"I bet she ate berries," said Dan.

I didn't pity the ailing beast. There was supposed to be a colt by now and there was not.

Pap drew a bottle from his hip pocket. Speaking to Mother, he said, "The herb doctor sent you a bottle of his tonic. Swore it would redden the blood and quicken the appetite."

"Mmm," Mother responded. She wouldn't have tasted it for a gold diamond.

Pap held the bottle against the light. "If this would arouse hunger, I'd dose the young'uns, the traps, and the mare. They say that when the unwell take to eating, they're on the mend. A sure sign."

"Old plug mare," I mumbled. I spoke aloud, "The herb doctor has a healthy nag. Not much bigger'n a colt. Was she mine, I'd not swap her for riches."

"I examined the pony's mouth," Pap said. "She's as old as Methuselum's grandpappy's uncle. Teeth worn to the gums. The doc's wife had the pony eating out of her hand. If a woman hasn't a child to spoil, she'll pet on a critter."

The baby waked suddenly, crying. Pap leaned over Mother's shoulder. He plucked the baby's chin. "I see blue eyes," he said. And he said, "This little chub even cries sweet."

I said, "I'd rather to hear a hooty owl hoot."

"Woe, woe," Pap moaned. "I reckon we might as well give the baby to the herb doctor's woman and be done. She has nothing to pamper except that agey nag and an old husband."

I looked at Holly. "I have an idee where your hidey place is," I said. "I aim to find it."

Said Holly, brushing hair out of her eyes, "It's hid too good. You can't." But she was uneasy. "Fool around my playhouse and you'll wish to your heart you hadn't."

Mother sighed. "If a pot of soup could be made tomorrow, I believe I could eat. Soup with a light seasoning." She rocked her chair impatiently as Holly and I kept bickering. "I can hardly wait to begin straightening out these children," she said.

"My opinion," Pap said, "you'll first have to comb their heads with a wagon wheel."

The mulberries were dead ripe. They hung like caterpillars, falling at a touch. I sat high in the tree among the zizzing locusts, longing to taste the berries and watching Holly. I saw her crawl under the house. I saw her skitter up the barn loft ladder. She went here and yon, and never could a body tell where.

I hurried toward the mill. The cow tunnels winding through the high growth of vine and weed in the bottom were empty. I listened. A beetle bug snapped. A bird made a clinky sound. I heard digging. Something went *rutch rutch.* I tiptoed toward the noise. There amid tall briars the herb doctor knelt, digging mayapple roots. The top of his bare head was glassy in the sun.

"Did some'un go this way?" I inquired.

The herb doctor paused. Sweat beaded his forehead. "A half-hour ago a skunk came within smelling distance. I had to stopple my nose a minute." He sorted the roots, pressing them between thumb and forefinger until the sap oozed. He frowned. "It's a mite late in the season to be gathering herbs, yet a kettle of tonic has to be brewed before we leave tomorrow." He plucked a wilted leaf from his shirt pocket. "I'm digging mayapple, but what I need is more of this boneset."

"I know where there's a patch," I said. "A whole big lot."

His brow smoothed. "Lead me to it, and I'll be mightily obliged."

I cut my eyes about, ashamed to say the thing I wanted. I ventured at last, "Would you be in a notion to swap your nag to our mare? I always did want an animal to my size."

"For seven years we've fed that pony," the herb doctor explained. "My wife thinks more of her than she does me. Well, close to it. She would scalp me, did I trade."

I grumbled, "Our animal will never have a colt like was promised."

The herb doctor stood up. He looked wise as a lawyer. "Your mare requires special medicine," he said. "I mix a tonic which cures any ill, brings to health man or beast." He clapped hands together to free the dirt. "I'll make a trade with you. Show me the boneset, and I'll give you the last bottle left."

I said, "I bet was a person to eat mulberries, some of that tonic would kill the poison."

"Cure anything."

A woman's voice called from the mill. "Oh, Doc! Doc, come here!"

The doctor started off, saying, "Wait till I see what the wife wants." When he returned, the cow tunnels were filled with his chortling. "That devil pony of ours!" he said, shaking with merriment. "You never know what she's up to. Well, sir, she guaranteed we'll leave tomorrow."

In late afternoon we stood by the mill with a poke crammed to the mouth with roots. The fragrance of cooking arose from their oven. I was wholly starved. The herb doctor said, "I'll fetch your pay," and brought out a bottle of medicine. "It's as strong as Samson," he said. And he said, "My wife's fixing something for your mother."

"Will it work?" I questioned, sliding the bottle into a pocket.

"It will fix up your mare and any other ill you can name."

The pony came from the rear of the millhouse. She stuck her head in at the door and drew back, crunching an apple. The herb doctor sniggered. "See that there? She's rotten petted."

"My colt is going to have people sense, too," said I.

"The pony is bound to stick her nose in where it oughten to be," the herb doctor said. His face wrinkled joyfully. The crown of his head shone. "What do you imagine she found this morning? We couldn't believe our eyes."

"What—what was it?" I longed to know.

The herb doctor sobered. "For a reason you'll understand later we don't want the place disturbed until we're gone."

"Where was it?"

"Will you promise not to peep until we're on the road?"

I promised.

"It's yonder," he said, pointing to the lower side of the millhouse where the floor rested on high posts. "Not a wonder your sister tried to scare us with tales of spiders and lizards. Aye, she's a wild one."

The doctor's wife brought a bowl capped with a lid. The plaits of her hair tipped her shoulders, and her eyes were as sad as a ewe's. "Suppose we could borrow a child from your parents?" she said. "Four children in your house, a mere one wouldn't be missed."

I had no answer for that.

The woman gave the bowl to me. "Take this mulberry cobbler to your mother. Tell her every berry has been inspected. Tell her they're healthy to eat."

I ran home, and my heart pounded as I went.

Mother sat with the baby. Pap stirred soup on the

kitchen stove, and Dan stood by him. I uncovered the cobbler and handed the bowl to Mother. A fruity smell lifted from it. My mouth watered. I had to speak loudly, for Mother had plugs of wool in her ears to dim the cry of locusts. I said what the herb doctor's wife told me to say. We heard Pap and Dan coming, and Mother whispered quickly, "We can't trust eating berries this year. Feed it to the chickens, and say nothing." There was only time to shove the dish under the bed.

Pap said, "Hasn't the locusts' crying spell about run its season?"

"This is the day they're accounted to quit," Mother answered.

Dan peeked at the baby nursing. He was bad jealous. He dropped to his knees and scampered under the bed.

Pap faced me. "I've looked up our mare in the book. One more page to turn, and out the window it flies."

I had lost faith. Anyhow, Pap was big to tease. On a level with Uncle Jolly, mighty near.

When I could recover the bowl to sneak it out of the house, I found it empty. Dan had gobbled the whole pie. How fearful I was, believing him in danger. I recalled my bottle of medicine. Could I persuade him to swallow a dose? A thought sprang into my head. I would dose all— the mare, Mother, and Dan.

I hastened to the barn and poured a fourth of the tonic into a scoop of oats. The mare poked her great tongue into the grain and ate it all. She was mighty fat already. On I footed to the house. I tipped into the kitchen. The soup pot was boiling on the stove, and I emptied all save one draft of the medicine into it. I kept a single swallow.

Holly came through the door as I pocketed the bottle.

She spoke angrily, "I heard the herb doctor tell you where my play place is. If you go there, something will scare your gizzard out."

"Huh," I said, mockingly.

The locusts hushed that very day. The next morning Sporty Creek was quiet as the first day of the world. It was so still I could hear the *neep* of crickets in the grass.

Before the dew dried, I hid in the bottom, waiting for the herb doctor and his wife to depart. I saw them load stove and mattress and chairs and trunk into their wagon.

They hitched up the pony and drove uphill to our house. I saw Pap and Mother shake their hands in farewell. I saw the doctor's wife pat the baby's head. Dan was there, but not Holly.

I crept to the lower side of the millhouse where the floor stood high. I crawdabbed under. There was nothing to see except four posts supporting the mill and an empty pan on the ground. I heard footsteps and hid behind a post.

Holly came underneath the floor with a cup of milk and crumbs of meat. She had the bait from Pap's varmint traps. And behold! Her hair was combed slick. Two long plaits tipped her shoulders.

Holly poured the milk into the pan. Squatting beside it, she called, "Rolly, holy, poley." Four small polecats came walking to lap the milk. Two big polecats came to nibble the meat. I blinked and could hardly credence my sight. Of a sudden the critters knew I was there. And Holly knew. The polecats vanished like weasel smoke.

Holly said not a word for a minute. She squatted pale and vengeful, narrowing her eyes at me. She spoke presently, and the words came cold and measured through tight lips. "The baby has been took," she said. "Poppy gave it to the doctor's wife."

I stood frozen. My breath caught. Pain coursed my chest as from a blow.

When I could move, I raced toward the house, speeding with loss aching inside of me.

I thrust my head in at the door. Pap had his knife out and was making a whimmy-diddle* for Dan. Mother was eating soup with bread crumbled in. The baby was nowhere to be seen. Mother was saying, "The soup—it has a queer whang. Still, things don't taste the same when you're puny." Dan's bowl was beside him on the floor, empty.

Seeing me, Pap grinned and said, "I'm closing the book on the mare. Tomorrow is about the day for the foal to get here. That's for sure."

"The baby!" I choked. "He's been took."

"Baby?" Pap puzzled. "Why, here he kicks on the bed, growing bigger than the government."

I turned, running away in shame and joy. I ran out to the mulberry tree. The fruit had fallen, and the ground was like a great pie. I drew the tonic bottle from my pocket and drained it. I ate a bellyful of mulberries.

---

*whimmy-diddle: toy whittled from a tree prong, also anything of small worth

7

the dumb-bull

Aaron Proffit drove a bunch of yearlings into our yard on a cold March evening. It was the very week Cass Logan sent word to Pap he needed a sawyer. Heifers bawled, and young bullies rattled the dark with their bellows. We hurried out onto the porch to learn what was afoot. As Aaron rode up to the doorsteps, Pap hailed him, not recognizing him at first. "Hey-o?" Pap called in uncertainty and, when he recognized Aaron, shouted heartily, "Alight and show your saddle!" Aaron was a penhooker. He was a skinflint to boot. Those who had been stung by him in a trade called him Dude.

Aaron opened his fleeced collar, rustling new leather. His breath curled into a fog. "If Sporty Creek mud gets any deeper," he grumbled, "it'll be beyond treading. In some spots my horse bogged to the knees."

"Any day now we'll see spring," Pap predicted. "It's time for her to explode. Then we can walk the earth and not sink."

Pap turned out our mare and colt and stalled Aaron's horse. My colt had finally showed up. He brought the brass-trimmed saddle onto the porch. Aaron shook his boots and scraped the caked mud upon the doorsteps.

Supper having long been eaten, Mother prepared a meal for Aaron.

Aaron shucked off his coat. A foam of sheep's wool lined the underside. "There's not a cent in yearlings," he said. "Hit's swapping copper for brass. Beef steers are what puts sugar in the gourd, and I've found not a single one between here and the head of Left Hand Fork."

"Crate Thompson cleaned the steers out of all the hollows on Sporty and over on Troublesome Creek in Knott County a month ago," Pap said, "and I've heard a sketch he's over on Quicksand Creek, buying in the Decoy and Handshoe neighborhoods."

Mother brought a plate of shucky beans, buttered cushaw,* and a sour-sweet nubbin of pickled corn. Holly raked coals upon the hearth for the coffeepot. While Aaron ate, Pap and me and Dan brightened Aaron's boots. We scraped the dirt away, rubbed on tallow, and spat on the leather. We polished them with rags until they glowed.

"I never saw boots have such razor toes," Pap said. "You could nigh pick a splinter out of your finger with them." He thrust forth his own to show the bluntness of the shoecaps. Pap's were the shape of the box they came in.

Pap picked up one of Aaron's boots and compared it to his shoe. "They have the difference of a hoe and a pickax," he said, sighing in awe. "Man! They must stack your toes into a pile."

Aaron champed his tobacco cud. "They're comfortable," he said.

On finishing his meal, Aaron said, "I'd take a shortcut to Quicksand if I didn't have the yearlings on my hands. Maybe I could get there before Crate Thompson cleans

---

*cushaw: winter squash

out the last beef animal." He rubbed the stubble of his chin. "Reckon your eldest boy here could drive the calves to Mayho town for me? That would save a whole day."

I raised off my chair, hoping. In another month I would be ten, to my mind agey enough to be trusted, to be allowed to venture into the world.

Pap hesitated.

"That's a right smart little chunk of a distance for a boy to walk alone. And I might be gone when he gets back. Expect to hit a few licks of work at Plank Town this spring."

"I'll pay him a dollar," Aaron said, "and I'll make it silver. Silas McJunkin's boy will be at my house to help with the penning, and my woman will settle with the both. Silas' boy is driving two cows from the mouth of Augland in the morning."

I thought, *I'm liable to be a cattleman when I grow up and travel far. I'll wear a fleecy jacket, and a belt three inches wide, and fancy boots.*

Mother sent Holly and Dan to bed. The baby was already in the quilts. Before going herself, she brought in a washpan and a ball of soap. Pap poured hot water from the kettle, and Aaron washed his face and hands, then pulled off his boots and socks and soaked his feet. His feet were white as milk. His heels bore no sign of ground-in dirt like ours.

I set off behind the yearlings at daybreak, and I had reached the mouth of Steer Fork and turned down Troublesome by the hour the sun-ball appeared above the ridge. The yearlings pitted the mud with their hooves, and I oft sank to my shoelaces. My breeches legs were splattered; my feet got stony cold. A wintry draft numbed my ears and nose. Yet the willows looked expectant, ready to leaf. The air smelled of rising sap.

The yearlings nearly ran my legs off. They dawdled, or they bunched, or they scattered. Anything to plague me. They made the most of my inexperience. I herded the day long, trotting right, racing left, reversing track, understanding then the work of a penhooker. And I gloried in it. I savored the sting of the weather, the waywardness of the calves. I relished being master.

Chimney sweeps★ were funneling the sky when I rounded the yearlings into Aaron Proffit's place. Dusk crept into Mayho by three roads, coming to sit among the sixteen homeseats crowding the creek or hanging off the hillsides. I saw Pud, Silas McJunkin's son, atop a fence post, nibbling a straw. He was about fifteen and man-tall. His hair shagged over his collar and hid his ears. He was as muddy as I. Pud helped pen the calves, and I got a whole look at Mayho before night blacked everything.

We beat on the Proffits' kitchen door. Aaron's woman opened it a crack, but we didn't cross the sill, for she saw our muddy clothes and told us to sleep in the barn. She poked out a dish of hand-pies† and a raggedy quilt. When we asked about our pay, the money Aaron had told us she would hand over, she said Aaron was on Quicksand and had sent word for us to come help him drive. He would settle with us then and pay double. And she said she would hurry word to my folk where I was by the first person going the road.

We ate the pies in the barn loft. We burrowed into the hay, leaving only our heads sticking out. Frosty as the night was, we shunned the quilt. Pud said, "Aaron's old hen had to shake the mice out to offer it."

I hated to lose the dollar, and the chance of two dollars

★chimney sweep: chimney swift
†hand-pie: hand-shaped pie with fruit filling

tempted me. Yet I said, "My folks would be worried if I didn't come straight home. Especially with Pap off to Logan's sawmill."

"Aaron has us over a barrel," Pud said. "Let's go drive for him and see he comes across with what's due. He's a tightwad, I've allus heard. Yet he won't skin us. No, sirreebob! One fashion or another, we'll see our money."

"I ought to light out for home," I said. "I plumb ought to." But I didn't.

We came on Aaron Proffit a half mile up Lower Quicksand Creek at Tom Zeek Duffey's place. He was expecting us and had already rounded four prime steers into Tom Zeek's barn lot. He kicked the board fence, testing the lot's tightness. The fence was weak. He said, "I figure I've put the cat on Crate Thompson, wherever he is. He's trading slow, like he had eternity and no competition. I aim to clean the beef out of this valley in three days and leave him the pickovers."

Tom Zeek's woman called us to supper. Not a bite had passed our lips that day, except for a robbing of chestnuts from a squirrel's nest and the sharing of a hunk of corn bread Pud had carried for two days in his pocket. The table held fourteen different dishes, and Pud and I ate some of everything. We drank buttermilk so thick a duck couldn't have paddled it. We stayed the night, sleeping deep in a goose-feather tick.

The next morning Aaron rousted us before daylight. Tom Zeek Duffey's woman fed us slabs of ham, scrambled eggs and locust honey, and flour biscuits the size of saucers. We set off, with Aaron leading.

Aaron bargained and bought the day long. We slept on the cold puncheon floor of a sawmill near Handshoe that night, with the boiler fired for heat. For supper and breakfast we ate pinfish* out of flat cans Aaron got at the Elmrock store. We started downcreek again, and where it had taken one day to go up, we spent two gathering the cattle and herding them to Tom Zeek's. Pud and I ran hollering and whooping in the burgeoning air.

We rounded eighteen steers and seven yearlings into Tom Zeek Duffey's lot. Tom Zeek told us Crate Thompson was across the gap, at John Adair's, hardly a mile away. "Hit mighty nigh cankered his liver when he learnt he'd been beat out," he said and, winking at me and Pud, added dryly, "Crate started trading soon enough, but what he lacked was a pair of sharp-toed seven-mile boots."

Aaron grinned. We chortled.

Said Aaron, "I aimed to singe his whiskers, and I done it."

Tom Zeek Duffey's lot was packed with cattle. The lot was roomy enough for a cow or two, a horse or so, but not for a drove of beef steers. Aaron drove extra nails in the board fence. He stretched barbed wire along the tops of the posts, and he sent for Tom Zeek's son-in-law to come help drive the herd to the railroad siding at Jackson the next day. He had no further need of Pud and me. He declared, "I wouldn't trust this pen more than a single night. Too cramped, too flimsy."

"Why not take these boys on to Jackson?" Tom Zeek suggested. "Provide a trip for them out into the world and an opportunity to spend the money they've worked out."

"These tadwhackers, no!" Aaron blared. "They would scare worse than a deer at the sight of a train engine. And if Pud walked the Jackson streets with that shaggy head, they'd muzzle him for a sheep dog."

---

*pinfish: sardines

Pud sneered, "My hair hain't so long you can step on it with your finicky boots. Anyhow, hit's pay time. Let us see your wallet."

"I'm out of pocket at the moment," Aaron said, unabashed at showing himself a miser before Tom Zeek. "Cash on the barrelhead I had to pay for the cattle."

"Well, sir, I'm setting me up a barrel."

"I'm broke teetotal," Aaron argued. "I won't have money to settle with you until the cattle are sold, so I've figured you two would be satisfied with a small yearling for pay—one between the both." `

"You aim to fill your gourd and leave ours empty," scoffed Pud. "We're not in the calf business. Hand over what we've earnt, or you'll wish to your stingy heart you had."

"A small yearling for you boys, or you'll have to wait. I can't come up with what I haven't got."

"Gosh-dog!" Pud swore angrily. "I hope every bull and cow and calf you own dies of the hollow tail."

Tom Zeek chided Aaron, "I like to see boys right-treated. Make fair weather with them if you can."

"I've made them a good offer," Aaron replied. "Youngsters their age wouldn't know what to do with money did they have it. They'd throw it to the wind."

Pud walked gloomily behind the barn, and I tagged along. He fished a wad of tobacco leaf from a hip pocket, chewed, and spat black on the dry stalks. "I'm one jasper Dude Proffit hain't going to cheat," he said.

"He put the cat on Crate Thompson and is proud of it," I said. "Now he'll brag he slicked one on us."

Pud snorted suddenly. "I'm of a mind to go talk to Crate," he blurted. "Crate Thompson being sore as a gumboil at Aaron, he might know what we should do." He brightened, and he blew the cud against the barn wall hard enough to make it stick. He strode into the barn and fetched out the mule shears.

I cut Pud's hair. I cut the locks bunched on his neck, the brush hiding his ears, the thicket on top of his head. I clipped and gaped and banged his head all over.

"I feel most nigh naked," Pud said when I had finished. "Wish I had me a looking glass to see in."

After dark we crossed the high gap to John Adair's home place. John and his woman were outside, milking and feeding stock. Crate Thompson sat before the hearth, driving sprigs* into a shoe sole. The shoe was a common old anybody's shoe, and not a proper penhooker's. Crate was as hefty as any of Aaron's steers.

"Draw up chairs," Crate said, speaking with lips tight so as not to swallow the sprigs in his mouth. His eyes were intent on Pud's cropped head. Pud sat down, but I remained standing, awkward and restive. If Crate remembered me from his cattle-buying trips along Sporty, he didn't show it.

Pud told Crate our trouble. Crate dropped the shoe, listening with a stub finger sunk into the bag of his chin.

"Where has Dude got the cattle penned?" Crate asked, his words issuing between the sprigs.

"In Tom Zeek Duffey's lot."

Crate spat the sprigs into a hand. Through his gray eyes a body could almost see ideas working in his skull. "Well, now," he spoke slowly, "I can't think of anything save a dumb-bull to cure Dude Aaron."

"Dumb-bull!" Pud cried in awe.

Crate's great chin quivered in pleasure. "Two nails, a leather string, a twine cord and a hollow log are the whole works." He paused, jabbing himself. "But I'll have no hand in it."

"I'll build my own bull fiddle," Pud said happily. "I

---

*sprig: tack

know how they're made. Hit's just tick-tacking* on a big scale."

"There's a law against them," Crate reminded.

"Who gives a hoot?"

"There are fellows roosting in the jailhouse for less."

"I'm not aiming to be skinned."

"Ah," Crate uttered, eyeing Pud's head. "A fine scalping you've had already."

Pud snickered.

Crate said, breathing satisfaction, "John should have a hide string hereabouts and some beeswax to grease it." He shuffled out of the room to locate them.

"I'm scared to do it," I told Pud. "I'm scared to tick-tack."

"We'll have Dude Aaron calling on his Maker," Pud declared.

"I ought to be going home," I said.

Pud fashioned the dumb-bull on the ridge above Tom Zeek Duffey's barn where the woods had been timbered and hollow logs were plentiful. The rising moon had the shape of a grass hook, just right according to Pud. Too much light would have been a drawback. Pud kicked trunk after fallen trunk until one resounded from the blow. A winged creature fluttered out, beating the chilly air. It complained overhead, *Ou? Ou?*

"Screech owl," Pud said.

Pud set to work on the dumb-bull. He drove twenty-penny nails at the ends of the crack in the log. He cut notch holes in the tip ends of the hide string and stretched it taut over the nailheads. My job was to wax

---

*tick-tacking: bowing a taut waxed cord to produce an eerie noise

the string of hide while he patterned a bow of a hickory sprout and the twine cord.

We perched on the log, waiting for the cattle to settle for the night. Although we couldn't see them under the hill, we heard them moving in the crowded lot. The steers were tramping restlessly, the yearlings bawling.

Presently Pud said, "Aaron has dropped his boots by now, and I'd bet my thumb the toes stuck up in the floor like jackknives."

A bird chirped sleepily near us.

"I'm freezing," I said. Anxiety burned cold as foxfire inside of me. "Let's kindle a little fire. They won't spot us."

"No need," Pud said. "We're a short time here. I'm only waiting until the brutes quiet. My opinion, it's best to catch 'em napping."

I made talk, hungry for company. I asked, "What are the towns of Jackson and Hazard like?" My teeth chattered.

Pud chewed a sliver of bark. "Folks wear their Sunday clothes on weeky days," he explained. "Their houses are so close together they can shake hands out of the windows."

"I aim to see both someday," I said. "I plan to. I've lived in a mine camp, but it wasn't a real town. A bunch of houses in a hollow."

"I've traveled a sight," Pud related. "I vow I've been near to the earth's end. Once I went to Glamorgan, in Old Virginia. Hain't that going somewheres?"

I nodded in the dark, remembering Mayho, the chimney sweeps riding the sky. I thought, *I've already seen Mayho town, and I've been on Quicksand Creek. That's far traveling.*

After a while Pud said, "I'd bet Crate Thompson was planning to tick-tack himself, he thought of it so quick.

And he had the hide string, cord, and nails too handy."

"Unh-unh," I disagreed. "A man of his weight couldn't climb this hill." If Sula Basham was the tallest being earthly, Crate appeared to me the hugest.

We hushed and waited. I dozed.

A rooster crowed midnight, and Pud jumped to his feet. "Hit's time to witch the steers," he said, shaking me. I trembled with dread and cold. I was numb and stiff, and I yearned for home. Pud dragged the hickory bow lightly across the dumb-bull's single string, and the sound brought me fully awake. It was like a wildcat's scream, long and blood-clotting and deafening. But that wasn't a patching to when Pud bore down. Then it wasn't a single wildcat. It was a woodsful, tearing each other's eyeballs out. It was Bedlam, hell broke loose. I believed the racket carried for miles.

Pud let up. The timber was alive with varmints. A squirrel tore through the trees, squawking. Wings flapped, and paws rattled underbrush. Below, in the barn lot, the steers bellowed. We could hear them charging the fence, crazy with fear. They butted the panels in anguish, and the ground rang with the thud of hooves. In their midst the yearlings bawled like the lost.

"We're not right-treating Tom Zeek Duffey," I said. "We oughtn't destroy his fence. He and his woman slept us and fed us good."

"We're doing Tom Zeek a favor," Pud said. "We're putting him in line for a new one." And he sawed the hide string again. Goose bumps raised on me. A scream came from the log like something fleeing Torment. We heard the fence give way, the boards trampled, the posts broken off. The steers lit out, bellowing and blowing, running upcreek and down, awaking creation.

Lamplight sprang into the windows of Tom Zeek Duffey's house. A door swung wide, and the shape of a man bearing a shotgun was outlined in the light. The gun lifted, steadied, and a spurt of flame leaped thundering. Birdshot rattled winter leaves below us.

"The dude can shoot a lead mine and still not touch us," Pud said. "Too far to up here." Yet it scared him, I'd say, as much as me. My legs wavered; my knees felt unworthy. Again the gun lifted, barrel angled higher, and discharged, and the earth within rods of us was peppered. When the gun made to fire a third time, Pud dropped his bow and ran full split, melting into the dark.

I ran too, trying to follow. I ran into a tree and fell stunned upon the ground. My head rang; sparks dazzled my eyes. When I got up, Pud was out of hearing, and there was no sound anywhere.

I crept on my hands and knees a long spell, for the moon had set and it was totally dark. I climbed upward, to the top of the ridge, skirting Tom Zeek Duffey's place, and descending to the creek on the lower side. I crept and walked for hours.

Daybreak came as I reached the valley floor. Spring birds were cutting up jack, bloodroot had poked up blossoms, and overnight the hills had taken on the color of greenback money. Where there had been mud two days before, there was hard earth, and a pleasure to walk upon. And standing in the road was a fat heifer. She gave a glad *moo* and trotted toward me. I let her get ahead. I drove her toward Sporty Creek. She looked to be sugar in my gourd, and a pair of thorn-toed boots on my feet, just like Aaron's.

When I got back to Sporty Creek, Pap was loading the wagon with our plunder to move to Plank Town. Uncle Jolly was to keep our cow and calf and my colt against the day we might return. The nanny as well.

8

plank town

We were living at Logan's camp when Uncle Jolly appeared on the plank road, heading toward our house. We hadn't seen him since spring. He arrived on an idle Thursday when only the loggers were at work, and folks sat visiting or being visited on porches. The mill operated three days a week. The saws were quiet, the steam boiler sighing instead of puffing. Smoke raised from the burning sawdust mountain as straight as a pencil.

Word had reached Uncle Jolly that Dan had lost two of his fingers and they needed transporting for burial on Sporty. The third and fourth fingers of Dan's left hand had been severed while he played at the mill. For Pap, who was already fed up with eight months of short workweeks, Dan's accident was the last button on Gabe's coat.*

Uncle Jolly came riding his anticky horse down the plank road with Jenny Peg prancing sideways. Upon sighting them, Pap announced, "Here comes the witty," and to make Dan brighten sang out:

---

*last button on Gabe's coat: deciding issue

The biggest fool you could ever seek
Dwells in the head of Sporty Creek;
He puts on his shirt over his coat,
Buttons his breeches around his throat.

Dan's face lightened. Since losing his fingers, he had become pampered beyond endurance. Any time Pap took seat he climbed onto his knees. He had turned into a worse pet than the baby.

The trick horse bowed. Jenny Peg bowed so low Uncle Jolly slid down her neck to the ground. He caught up Dan, sprang onto the animal's back, and circled the house before saying a *hey-o* or a *howdy-do* to us.

Everybody humored Dan. Although the bandage was long off, the edge of the palm healed, he still drew attention. My playfellows broke off their games to stare at him, to gaze at the stake in a corner of the yard where the fingers were interred in a baking powder can. We had visitors aplenty. Camp folk made our narrow porch their porch.

They came with gifts for Dan: chestnuts, hickory sugar,* trifles. Cass Logan, Pap's boss, was a regular caller, dropping in for a moment with popcorn or a trinket, flashing gold teeth, and saying, "There you are, little master." Cass was concerned that Pap might law† him.

Uncle Jolly swung Dan to Pap. Pap handled him as carefully as he might a basket of eggs. Teasing, Uncle Jolly inquired, "Does sawdust smell as sweet to you as coal dust?"

"The same difference," said Pap.

Sawmilling was as slack as mining, and on off days Pap

---

*hickory sugar: candy flavored with hickory bark
†law: sue

had taken to searching the woods for wild herbs. A string of ginseng roots hung from a nail on the porch wall.

To low-rate Uncle Jolly's farming, Pap went on, "Lumbering beats grubbing newground in February and pushing a hardtail* along a corn furrow in the heat of the gnats."†

"I'm hearing you," said Uncle Jolly, "but I'd bet my ears you'll be moving again. Here you are on your honkers in the middle of the week."

"He's talking it," said Mother.

"Yes, sir," admitted Pap. "The hawk appears about to light."

"A born gypsy if one ever walked the earth," breathed Uncle Jolly.

Then Uncle Jolly noticed me, and the baby, and Holly. To me he said, "Hey-o, dirty ears." I regretted not having on my sharp-toed boots. I was barefoot, hardening my soles for the winter. Of the baby he asked, "From what worm tree** did you shake this grub?" As many times as he had pranked with it on Sporty, he acted like he'd never glimpsed it before. He keened his eyes at Holly and said, "This young lady is still at home, ay? I'd of sworn some boy rooster would of crowed by now, and she'd of gone a-running."

Holly pitched her chin. "Silly," she scoffed, and turned her back.

Pap reproved her, "I wish you'd change your byword again. I'm getting burnt out on this'un." And to Uncle Jolly he said, "Speaking of matrimony, how's the wife hunt?"

---

*hardtail: mule
†heat of the gnats: midsummer, also work under compulsion
**worm tree: catalpa

"Courting to marry," chimed Uncle Jolly.

"You've been singing that tune a dozen years."

"The trouble is females don't trip over each other to get to me."

"The switchtail you sparked on Bee Branch four or five seasons—what's become of her?"

"She chose another." Uncle Jolly sighed. "And you know what? I was beginning to like the girl."

"*Like?*" Pap repeated. "Is that the right word?" His chest began to heave. "So you've run out of courting material."

Pap had to laugh a spell before he could go on.

Changing the subject, Uncle Jolly asked Mother, "Are you packing your plunder to move? I'm figuring you're not long for the saw camp."

"With everything in a slump," Mother replied, "it's my hope. It's up to Mr. Hard Skull."

Pap swept an arm toward the string of roots hanging on a nail. "Back to the Old Place some far day," he said, "but not the next go. I'm speculating on something."

Pap turned grave. "Know what ginseng roots fetch nowadays? Thirty-five dollars the pound, and rising. These I found hereabouts, and they're pea-jibbits* to what must grow in the wild place I told you about—the territory owned by a lumber company. Besides ginseng there's snakeroot and golden seal and wild ginger and a host of other medicine roots that haul in big prices."

"It's a nowhere place," said Uncle Jolly. "A nobody world."

"Hit's not altogether uninhabited," defended Pap. He was wound up. "There are scatterings of settlers on the outer boundary, and there's Kilgore post office. When

---

*pea-jibbit: small clay marble

the company lumbered it twenty years ago, they had their sawmill in what's named Tight Hollow. The bunkhouse is still standing, in dandy shape. Ay, I aim to talk to the lawyer in Thacker who has say-so over the property."

"They'll call it Dunce Hollow hereafter, if you move there. But I figure you're talking to hear your head rattle. Or you're dreaming."

"If he's asleep," pronounced Mother, "he'd better wake up."

Pap rushed on. "Stands to reason such a territory is crammed with herbs, the waters jumping with fish, the woods crawling with game. Minks and muskrats who've never smelled a steel trap." He paused, overcome by such prospects. "Have you an idea what a mink skin fetches in the market? A muskrat?"

Uncle Jolly shook his head. He appealed to Mother, "Are you certain your man hasn't been cracked on the noggin?"

Mother answered dolesomely, "He's given to bad judgment sometimes. I can't picture myself stuck in such a wilderness."

Holly said, "I don't aim to move a jillion miles from creation."

"I want to," I cried. "I do."

"Me, too," said Dan.

Uncle Jolly jerked his chin in my direction. "I'd of sworn you favored Sporty where you can plow."

"I do," said I.

"First you want to go crawl with the varmints?"

I thought about it. My mind spun. "I want to live everywhere," I said.

"And what is it you want to do in the world?"

I weighed that in my head. "Everything," I said. There was no other truth.

Uncle Jolly reached and tapped my head and listened. "Not quite as empty as it used to be. Something in there, a little something."

On the porch of the dwelling across the plank road, a neighbor began to pick a familiar song on his guitar. We could see the guitar player's head bobbing, his arm jerking. The Plunker, Pap had nicknamed him. Presently a girl of six or seven skipped into our yard with a stick of peppermint in her hand. She dropped it into Dan's lap and departed without a word.

"Dadburn!" Uncle Jolly swore. "Six years old and already drawing the women. Never saw the beat."

"The neighbors are ruining him," complained Mother. "He's so spoiled salt wouldn't save him."

"You've done your share," reminded Pap.

I scurried indoors and pulled on my sharp-toed boots. On returning, Uncle Jolly had the baby in his arms, counting its fingers. He tallied, "Thumbo, Lickpot, Long Man, Ring Man, Little Man." He wagged his chin in mock surprise. "I expected six." Then he glimpsed Dan hiding his crippled hand in a pocket.

"Golly Moses!" Uncle Jolly crowed. He surrendered the baby to Mother and declared, "Dan is in luck. With a pair of fingers short, the picks and shovels* won't get him, the army won't capture him. It opens up the world. My belief is he'll amount to a really something, something worth the candy.† Ay, he'll be a somebody."

I forgot the boots. They were nothing compared to this. To do something; to be somebody! I was half envious. Mother said quickly, "Yes," and again, "Yes."

"If Dan is to have a chance," Uncle Jolly said, "teach-

---

*picks and shovels: coal mine employment
†worth the candy: worth doing

ers such as Duncil Hargis and his sort won't help. And with school closed on Sporty, Buffalo Wallow is a far piece to walk. I say send him to the Settlement School at the forks of Troublesome Creek. There the scholars work out their room and board."

Dan pursed his lips. "I hain't a-going."

Uncle Jolly turned solemn. "Listen," said he. "The Settlement's teachers are the knowingest. They will do for you. They'll fit you for living in a hard world. Anyhow, the Buffalo Wallow teacher is a whip-jack.* He'll put the bud† to you. A bad sign."

Pouting, Dan snuffed, "I don't want to."

A cry raised on my tongue. "I do! I aim to!" Menifee Thomas, a Sporty Creeker, had told me a bushel about the Settlement.

"Send the both," Uncle Jolly said, and spying at me, he added, "When I tapped your head last, I heard more brains than I let on. Didn't want to get you stuck up."

He was staring at my boots as he spoke. He closed an eye, cracked it, and shut the other, acting as if he couldn't credence what he beheld. "I swear to my Never!" he blurted. "If I had a pair as good-looking as that, I could borrow money at the Thacker bank."

Pap explained, "They're his calf boots. Bought them out of his own pocket. First dollars earned." He sighed, feigning envy. "Wears better leather than his own pappy."

Pap's shoes were in sad shape. He bought for himself only when he had to.

---

*whip-jack: given to corporal punishment
†bud: hickory limb

9
tight hollow

We moved from Plank Town to Tight Hollow on a day in March when the sky was as gray as a war penny and wind whistled the creek roads. Pap had got himself appointed caretaker of the tract of timber he had long told us about, his wages free rent. He had made a quick trip in, returned to say nothing was lacking. He had talked to the people on Grassy Creek who were to be our closest neighbors.

Cass Logan took us in his truck. Pap rode in the cab with Cass, and every jolt made him chuckle. He laughed at Cass' complaint of the chugholes, and he teased him for holding us up a day in the belief we might change our minds. Beside them huddled Mother, the baby on her lap, her face dolesome. Holly and Dan and I sat on top of the load, and when a gust blew my hat away, I only grinned, for Pap had promised us squirrel caps. Holly was as set against moving as Mother. She hugged her cob dolls and pouted.

The tract lay beyond Marlett and Rough Break, and beyond Kilgore where the settlements ended—eleven thousand acres of forest. Although clear-cut years before, the woods had regenerated and trees were again nearly to saw timber size. It was Pap's belief that game would provide our meat, sugar maples our sweetening. Garden sass and corn would thrive in dirt as black as a shovel. Herbs and pelts would furnish ready cash.

Pap had thrown over his job, which had shrunk to a couple of days a week, and bought steel traps and gun shells and provisions, including a hundred-pound sack of pinto beans. At the last moment he even rented our mare to Cass. Mother held out against an outright sale. Pap had used the last dime without getting the new shoes he needed. He was still wearing the pack peddler pair. He told us, "Tight Hollow is a mite narrow as valleys go, but that's to our benefit. Cold blasts can't punish in winter; summers the sun won't tarry long enough overhead to sting. We can sit on our hands and rear back on our thumbs."

Once Pap had made up his mind, arguing was futile. Still, Mother had spent her opinion. "Footgear doesn't grow on bushes to my knowledge," she said.

"You tickle me." Pap had chuckled. "Why, ginseng roots alone bring thirty-five dollars a pound, and seneca and golden seal pay well. Mink hides sell for twenty dollars, muskrat up to five. Ay, we can buy shoes by the rack. We'll get along and hardly pop a sweat."

"Whoever heard of a fellow opening his hand and a living falling into it?" Mother asked bitterly.

Mother's lack of faith amused Pap. "I'll do a few dabs of work," he granted. "But mostly I'll stay home and grow up with my children. Kilgore post office will be the farthest I'll travel, and I'll go there only to ship herbs and hides and rake in the money." He poked his arms at the baby, saying, "Me and this little chub will end up the biggest buddies ever was. And I'll have the peace of mind to think him up a fitting name."

The baby strained toward Pap, but Dan edged between them.

Mother inquired, "What of a school? Is there one within walking distance?"

Holly pulled her cheeks and grumbled, "I'd bet it's a jillion miles to a neighbor's house."

"Schools are everywhere nowadays," Pap said, his face clouding. A school hadn't occurred to him.

"Bet you could look your eyeballs out," Holly said, "and see nary a soul."

Annoyed, Pap explained, "A family lives on Grassy Creek, several miles this side. Close enough to my notion. Too many tramplers kill a wild place."

"Plank Town is no paradise," Mother said, "but we have friendly neighbors and a school. We know the whereabouts of our next meal."

Pap wagged his head in irritation. He declared, "I'll locate a school by the July term, fear you not." And passing on, he said, "Any morning I can spring out of bed and slay a mess of squirrels. We'll eat squirrel gravy that won't quit. Of the furs we'll pattern caps for these young-'uns, leaving the tails on for handles."

Mother sighed and asked, "When you've learned we can't live like foxes, will you bow to the truth? Or will you hang on until we starve out?"

Of a sudden Pap slapped his leg so hard he startled the baby and made Dan jump. "Women aim to have their way," he blurted. "One fashion or another they'll get it. They'll burn the waters of the creek, if that's what it takes. They'll upend creation."

Daylight was perishing when we turned into Tight Hollow. The road was barely a trace. The tie rods dragged. Cass groaned, and Pap chuckled. The ridges broke the wind, though we could hear it hooting in the lofty woods. Three-quarters of a mile along the branch the sawmill and the bunkhouse came to view, and unaccountably, smoke rose from the bunkhouse chimney. The door hung ajar, and as we drew up, we saw fire smoldering on the hearth.

Nobody stirred for a moment. We could not think how this might be. Father called a *hey-o* and got no reply. Then he and Cass strode to the door. They found the building empty save for a row of kegs and an alder broom. They stood wondering.

Cass said, "By the size of the log butts I judge the fire was built yesterday."

"Appears a passing hunter slept here last night," Pap guessed.

We unloaded the truck in haste, Cass being anxious to start home. Dan and I kept at Pap's heels, and Holly tended the baby and her dolls, the while peering uneasily over her shoulder. Our belongings seemed few in the lengthy room, and despite lamp and firelight, the corners were gloomy.

At leaving, Cass informed Pap, "I haven't told you before, but here's the lowdown. My mill has to close next month for lack of orders. Otherwise I'd have refused to haul you to such a godforsaken area."

Pap grinned. The moving was now justified in his eyes.

Cass went on, "When you tire of playing wild man, let me hear. I'll haul you to Sporty Creek or as near to your Old Place as I can get. I'll keep the mare for you and use her for my gin work." And he twitted, "Don't stay till Old Jack Somebody carries you off plumb. He's the gent, my opinion, who lit your fire."

"I pity you working stiffs," Pap bantered. "You'll slave, you'll drudge, you'll wear your fingers to nubs for what Providence offers as a bounty."

"You heard me," Cass Logan said, and drove away.

The bunkhouse had no flue to accommodate the stove-pipe, and Mother cooked supper on coals raked onto the hearth. The bread baked in a skillet was round as a grindstone. Though we ate little, Pap advised, "Save space for a stout breakfast. Come daybreak I'll be gathering in the squirrels."

Dan and Holly and I pushed aside our plates. We gazed at the moss of soot riding the chimney back, the fire built by we knew not whom. We missed the sighing of the sawmill boilers. We longed for Logan's camp. Mother said nothing, and Pap fell silent. Presently Pap yawned and said, "Let's fly up if I'm to rise early."

Lying big-eyed in the dark, I heard Pap say to Mother, "That fire puzzles me. Had we come yesterday as I planned, I'd know the mister to thank."

"You're taking it as seriously as the young'uns," Mother answered. "I believe to my heart you're scary."

When I waked the next morning, Mother was nursing the baby by the hearth and Holly was warming her dolls. Dan waddled in a great pair of boots he had found in a keg. The wind had quieted, the weather grown bitter. The cracks invited freezing air. Father was expected at any moment, and a skillet of grease simmered in readiness for the squirrels.

We waited the morning through. Toward ten o'clock we opened the door and looked upcreek and down, seeing by broad day how prisoned was Tight Hollow. The ridges crowded close. A body had to tilt head to see the sky. At eleven, after the sun had finally topped the hills, Mother made hobby bread* and fried rashers† of salt

---

*hobby bread: bread baked in a slab
†rasher: slice of meat

meat. Bending over the hearth, she cast baleful glances at her idle stove. Pap arrived past one, and he came empty-handed and grinning sheepishly.

"Game won't stir in such weather," he declared. "It'd freeze the clapper in a cowbell." Thawing his icy hands and feet, he said, "Just you wait till spring opens. I'll get up with the squirrels. I'll pack the gentlemen in. Then you can break out Old Huldey."*

The cold held. The ground was iron, and spears of ice the size of a leg hung from the cliffs. The bunkhouse was drafty as a basket, and we turned like flutter mills before the fire. We slept under a burden of quilts. And how homesick we children were for the whine of gang saws, the whistle blowing noon! We yearned for our playfellows. Holly sulked. She sat by the hearth and attended her dolls.

Pap set up his trap line along the branch and then started a search for sugar trees and game. There was scarcely a maple to be found. "Sweetening rots teeth anyhow," he told us. "What sugar we need we can buy later." Hunting and trapping kept him gone daylight to dark, and he explained, "It takes hustling at the outset. But after things get rolling, Granny Nature will pull the main haul. I'll have my barrel full of resting."

When Pap caught nothing in his traps two weeks running, he made excuse. "You can't fool a mink or a muskrat the first crack. The newness will have to wear off the iron." And for all the hunting, my head went begging a cap. Rabbits alone stirred. Tight Hollow turned out pesky with rabbits. "It's the weather that has the squirrels holed," he said.

---

*Old Huldey: common name for a skillet

"Maybe there's a lack of mast trees,"★ Mother said. "Critters have sense enough to live where there's food to be had. More than can be said for some people I know."

Pap squirmed. "Have a grain of patience," he ordered. To stop the talk he said, "Fetch the baby to me. I want to start buddying with the little master. I might even think up a right name for him."

During March, Dan and I nearly drove Mother distracted. We made the bunkhouse thunder. We went clumping in the castaway boots. The abandoned sawmill beckoned, but the air was too keen, and we dared not venture much beyond the threshold. Often we peered through cracks to see if Old Jack Somebody was about, and at night I tied my big toe to Dan's so should either of us be snatched in sleep the other would wake.

Within a month's time we used more than half of the cornmeal and most of the lard. The salt meat shrank. The potatoes left were spared for seed. When the coffee gave out, Pap posed, "Now, what would Old Dan'l Boone have done in such a pickle?" He bade Mother roast pintos and brew them. But he couldn't help twisting his mouth every swallow. Rabbits and beans we had in plenty, and Pap assured, "They'll feed us until the garden sass crosses the table." Holly grew thin as a sawhorse. She claimed beans stuck in her throat and professed to despise rabbit. She lived on broth.

The traps stayed empty, and Pap said, "Fooling a mink is ticklish business. The idea is to rid the suspicion and set a strong temptation." He baited with meat skins, rancid grease, and rabbit ears. He boiled the traps, smoked them, even buried them awhile. "I'll pinch toes yet," he vowed, "doubt you not."

★mast trees: trees producing nuts

"The shape your feet are in," Mother remarked, "the quicker, the better."

"We're not entirely beholden to pelts," Pap hedged. "Even if I had the bad luck to catch nothing, the herbs are ahead of us—ginseng at thirty-five dollars a pound."

"I doubt your shoes will hold out to tread grass," said Mother.

Coming in with nothing to show was awkward for Pap, and he teased or complained to cover his embarrassment. One day he saw me wearing a stocking cap Mother had made, and he laughed fit to choke. Again, spying Holly stitching a tiny garment, he appealed to Mother, "Upon my deed! Eleven years old and pranking with dolls. I recollect when girls her age were fair on to becoming young women."

"Away from other girls," Mother remarked, "how can she occupy herself?"

"Stir about," said Pap, "not mope."

Holly said, "I'm scared to go outside. Every night I hear a booger."

"So that's it," Pap scoffed.

Mother abetted Holly, "Something waked me an evening or so ago. A rambling noise, a walking sound."

"My opinion," Pap said, "you heard a tree frog or a hooty owl. Leave it to women to build a haystack of a single straw. Stuff your ears nights, you two, and you'll sleep better."

The cold slackened early in April. It rained a week. The spears of ice along the cliffs plunged to earth, and the branch flooded. The waters covered the lumberyard of the sawmill, lapped under the bunkhouse floor, filled the hollow wall to wall. They swept away Pap's traps. When the skies cleared, there was not a solitary trap to be discovered.

"Never you fret," Pap promised Mother, "herbs will provide. I've heard speak of families of ginseng diggers roaming the hills, free as the birds. They made a life of it."

"I'd put small dependence in such tales," Mother said.

The woods hurried into leaf. Dogwood and service bushes whitened the ridges, and wheedle-dees* called in the laurel. One morning Mother showed Pap strange tracks by the door. Pap stood in the tracks, and they were larger than his shoes. He wagged his head. The tracks were every whit the size of the boots found in the keg.

"My judgment," Mother said, "we're wanted begone. They're out to be rid of us. They aim to hound us off the tract."

"I'm the appointed caretaker of this scope of land," Pap replied testily, "and I'll not leave till I get my ready on."

Wild greens spelled the pintos and rabbit. We ate branch lettuce and ragged breeches and bird's-toe and swamp mustard. We went back to the beans and rabbit when the plants toughened. By late April the salt meat was down to rind, the meal sack more poke than bread, and the lard scanty. Pap hewed out a sass patch and then left the planting and tilling to Mother. He took up ginseng hunting altogether. He came in too weary to pick at us, and he rarely saw the baby awake. Dan began to look askance at him. As for his shoes, he was patching the patches.

One night Mother said to Pap, "My opinion, it's time to choose a name for the baby. High time. Name it and be done."

Pap said, "I've considered Sim. Sim Brannon helped

---

*wheedle-dee: wood thrush

us when we needed him. And I've considered Cass. Cass Logan has treated us well." He sighed, too tired to think. "A pitch-up."

Said Holly, "I don't like 'em."

"Me neither," said Dan.

I said naught. But for a baby with a cowlick and two crowns these names seemed unworthy. Mother had told us two crowns meant a noble life on this earth and an assurance of heaven.

Dan and I gradually forgot Old Jack. We waded in the branch and played at the sawmill. We pretended to work for Cass Logan. With poles for peaveys we rolled play logs, buzzing to match steel teeth eating timber. Dan's crippled hand was no hinder. And we chased cowbirds and rabbits out of the garden. Rich as the ground was, the seeds sprouted tardily, for the sun warmed the valley floor only at the height of the day. Mother fixed a scarecrow and dressed it in Pap's old clothes. We would hold the baby high and say, "Yonder's Pap! Pap-o!" The baby would stare as at a stranger.

Pap happened upon the first ginseng in May and bore it home proudly. We crowded to see it—even Holly. Three of the roots were forked and wrinkled, with arms and legs and a knot of a head. One had the shape of a spindle. Tired though he was, Pap boasted, "The easiest licks a man ever struck. Four digs, four roots."

"Dried they'll weigh like cork," Mother pronounced. She asked. "Why didn't you hit more taps, make the tramping worth the leather?"

His ears reddening, Pap stammered, "The stalks are barely breaking dirt. Hold your horses. You can't push nature."

Pap glanced about for the baby, thinking to skip an argument. The baby was asleep. He complained, "Is the chub going to slumber its life away?" He eyed Dan leaning against Mother and said, "That kid used to be a daddy's boy. Acted to be my 'possum baby.* Used to keep my knees rubbed sore." He took a square look at Holly and inquired, "What ails her? I want to know. She's nothing but skin and bones."

"You're the shikepoke," Mother replied. "You've walked yourself to a blade. If you came home earlier, you would find the baby wide-eyed."

The baby happened to be awake one evening—the evening we'll forever recall. The little one had pulled himself up by a chair or by a knee, yet had never walked. On this particular evening he hoisted himself, stood alone, and took the first tottering steps. In the garment made of my striped shirt he looked like a stick of candy. He fell. Up he came again, with no help, and waddled on. He headed toward none of us. He walked as independent as a hog on ice.

One day Pap arrived in the middle of the afternoon swinging two squirrels by the tails. He came grinning in spite of having found no ginseng. He crowed, "We'll allow the beans and the bunnies a vacation. We'll feast on squirrel gravy. Break out Old Huldey." Pap jiggled them to make the baby flick its eyes. It barely noticed, for it was playing with Mother's locket. After skinning the squirrels, Pap stretched the hides across boards and hung them to cure.

The gravy turned out grainy and tasteless. Lacking milk, and with bran substituted for flour, there was no help for it. Yet Pap smacked his lips. He offered the baby a spoonful, and it shrank away. He ladled Dan a serving, and Dan refused it. Tempting Holly, he urged, "Try a sop, and mind you don't swallow your tongue." Holly

---

*'possum baby: favored child

wrinkled her nose. "Take nourishment, my lady," he cajoled, "or you'll dry up and blow away."

"Humph!" Holly scoffed and left the table.

Pap's patience shortened. "Can't you make the young-'un eat?" he demanded of Mother. "She's wasting to a skeleton."

"We'll all lose flesh directly," Mother said.

Holly said, "Was I on Sporty, I'd eat a bushel."

Pap opened his mouth to speak but caught himself. He couldn't outtalk the both. He gritted his teeth and hushed.

When ginseng proved scarce and golden seal and seneca very scattering, Pap dug five-cent-a-pound dock and twenty-five-cent wild ginger. He dug cohosh and crane's bill and bluing weed and snakeroot. He worked like an ant. Mornings he left so early he carried a lantern to light his path, and he returned after we children had dozed off. Still, the bulk of herbs drying on the hearth hardly seemed to increase from day to day. Again Mother reported strange tracks, but Pap shrugged. "It's not the footprints that plague me," he said, "hit's the puzzle."

The sass patch failed. The corn dwarfed in the shade, the grains mere blisters on the cob. The tomatoes blighted. The potato vines were pale as though grown under thatch. We ate the last of the bread, and then we knew beans and rabbit plain. We must have all dreamed of the salt mackerel at Houndshell and the giant wheel of cheese. Pap hammered together box traps and baited for groundhogs, but the groundhogs were too wise for Pap.

Awaking one evening as Pap trudged in, I heard Mother say direfully, "We'll have to flee this hollow, no two ways talking. They'll halt at nothing to be rid of us."

"What now?" Pap asked wearily.

"Next they'll burn us out," Mother said, displaying a bunch of charred sticks. "Under the house I found these.

By a mercy the fire perished before the planks took spark."

"May have been there twenty years," Pap discounted. "Who knows how long?"

"Fresh as yesterday," Mother insisted. "Smell of them."

"To my thinking," Pap ridiculed, "scorched sticks and big tracks are awful weak antics. The pranks of some witty, some dumbhead."

"We can't risk guessing," Mother begged. "For the sake of the children—" She threw up her hands. "You're as stubborn as Old Billy Devil!" she cried.

Pap yawned. He was too exhausted to wrangle.

The day came when Pap's shoes wore out completely. He hobbled home at dusk and told Mother, "Roust the old boots that were found in the keg. My shoes have done all they came here to do."

"They'll swallow your feet," Mother objected. "They'll punish." She was close to tears.

"It's a force put," Pap said. "I'll have to use the pair even if they cost me a yard of skin."

Reluctantly Mother brought the boots, and Pap stuffed the toes with rags and drew them on. They were sizes too large and rattled as he walked. Noticing how gravely we children watched, he pranced to get a rise out of us. Our faces remained solemn.

"I'll suffer these till I can arrange otherwise," he said, "and that I aim to do shortly. I'll fetch the herbs to the Kilgore post office tomorrow."

"They may bring in enough to shod you," Mother said, "if you'll trade with another pack peddler." She dabbed her eyes. "A season's work not worth a good pair of shoes!"

His face reddening, Pap began sorting the herbs. But he couldn't find the ginseng. He searched the fireplace, the floor. He looked here and yon. He scattered the heaps. Then he spied Holly's dolls. The forked ginseng roots were clothed in tiny breeches, the spindle-shaped ones tricked in wee skirts. They were dressed like people. "Upon my deed!" he sputtered.

Pap paced the bunkhouse, the boots creaking. He glared at Holly, and she threw her neck haughtily. He neared Dan, and Dan sheltered behind Mother. He reached to gather up the baby, and it primped its face to cry. "Upon my word and deed and honor," he blurted, and grabbed his hat and the lantern. "Even the Grassy Creek folks wouldn't plumb cold-shoulder me. I'm of a notion to spend a night with them." He was across the threshold before Mother could speak to halt him.

Pap was gone two days, and Mother was distraught. She scrubbed the bunkhouse end to end. She mended garments and sewed on buttons. She slew every weed in the puny garden. When there was nothing more to do, she gathered up the squirrel skins and patterned caps.

The afternoon of the second day she told us, "I'm going downcreek a spell. Keep the baby company, and don't set foot outside." Taking Pap's rifle gun, she latched the door behind her.

We watched through cracks and saw her enter the garden and strip the scarecrow. We saw her march toward the mouth of the creek, gun in hand, garments balled under an arm. She returned presently, silent and empty-handed, and she sat idle until she saw Pap coming.

Pap arrived wearing new shoes and chuckling. I ran to meet him, the tail of my fur cap flying, and he had to chortle awhile before he could take another step. He chirruped, "Stay out of trees, mister boy, or you may be shot for a critter." But it wasn't my cap that had set him laughing. Upon seeing Mother, he drew his jaws straight.

He wore a dry countenance, though his eyes glittered.

Mother gazed at Pap's brand-new boots. They were as shiny as my own though the toes were not pointy. "How are the people on Grassy?" she asked.

"They're in health," Pap replied, hard put to master his lips. "And from them I got answers to a couple of long-hanging questions. I learned the location of the closest schoolhouse. I know who kindled the logs in our fireplace back yonder."

Dan, hiding behind Mother, thrust his head into view. Holly put aside her dolls and listened, and the baby widened its eyes. Then Pap greeted the baby. "Why, hello, Little Jolly," and that was the first we knew of its name.

Mother looked startled and pleased.

"I was stumped between Cass and Sim," Pap explained. "Couldn't choose one without slighting the other. So, as it appears Uncle Jolly will never have a namesake of his own, I've decided to furnish him one."

"Never give Jolly out," said Mother, brightening. "He may fool you."

Said Pap, "Fooling is the best thing he does." He blinked. He held himself in. "And he's not alone. Today I've met his match." And Pap went on with explanations. "Kilgore has the closest school. A mite farther away than I had counted on. So it's the Settlement School at the forks of Troublesome for the boys. They're to go right shortly, for I've signed 'em up. As for the fire, why, the Grassy man made it to welcome us the day he expected us to move here. Recollect we were a day late. But he's not the mischief who planted tracks and pitched burned sticks under the house. Nor the one who waylaid me at the mouth of the hollow while ago."

Mother cast down her eyes.

Pap went on, struggling not to laugh. "A good thing I made a deal with Cass Logan to haul our plunder to

Sporty. Ay, a piece of luck he paid me rent for our horse, and I could buy footgear to run in when I blundered into the ambush."

Mother lowered her head.

Swallowing, trying to contain his joy, Pap said, "Coming into the hollow, I spied a gun barrel pointing across a log at me—a gun plime-blank like my own. Behind a bush was a somebody rigged in my old coat and plug hat. Gee-o, did I travel!"

Mother raised her chin. Her eyes were damp, yet she was smiling. "If you'd stop carrying on," she said, "you could tell us how soon to expect Cass."

A gale of laughter broke in Pap's throat. He threshed the air. He fought for breath. "I can't," he gasped. "You've tickled me."

10

journey to the forks

"Hit's a far piece," Dan said. "I'm afraid we won't make it against dusty dark." We squatted down in the road and rested on the edge of a clay rut. Dan set his poke on the crust of a mule's track, and I lifted the budget off my shoulder. The cloth was damp underneath.

"We ought never thought to be scholars," Dan said.

The sun-ball had turned over the ridge above Gideon Whitfield's farm, and it was hot in the valley. Grackles walked the top rail of a fence, breathing with open beaks. They paused and looked at us, their legs wide apart and rusty backs arched.

"I figured you would get homesick before we reached the forks of Troublesome," I said. "I knowed it from the time we left Sporty."

Dan drew his thin legs together and propped his chin on his knees. "If I was growed up as old as you," he said, studying his toes, "I wouldn't care. I'd not mind my hand."

"Writing hain't done with your left hand," I said. "It won't get in the way of learning."

"I shouldn't of been playing at the sawmill," Dan said. "Two fingers gone is a hurting sight."

"By and by it will seem plumb natural," I said. "In a

little while they'll forget it. The scholars won't notice."

The grackles called harshly from the rail fence.

"We had better eat the apples while we're setting," I said. Uncle Jolly had given them to us when we stopped at his house for a drink of water in passing. "You take the Wilburn," I told him, for it was the largest. "I favor the Pippin because it pops when I bite it."

Dan wrapped the seeds in a scrap of paper torn from the poke. I got up, lifting the budget, a meal sack with our clothes in it.

"It's near on to six miles farther to the forks," I said. To spell me, Dan asked to carry the budget a ways. I told him, "The load would break you down." I did let him pack my calf boots. I had on my clodhoppers. He tied the strings into a bow and hung them with his own about his neck.

We trudged on, stepping among hardened clumps of mud and wheel-brightened rocks. Cow bells clanked in a redbud thicket on the hills, and a calf bellowed. A catbird mewed in a persimmon tree. I couldn't spot it, but Dan glimpsed it flicking its tail feathers. Dan was tiring now. He stumped his sore big toe twice, crying some each occasion.

"You'll have to stop dragging your feet or put on your shoes," I said.

"My feet would get raw as a beef if'n I wore shoes the whole trip," Dan declared. "Mine are full of pinchers. Did I have a drop of water on my toe, it would ease it."

Farther along we discovered a spring drip, and Dan held his foot under it. He wanted to skin up the bank to where the water seeped from the ground. "There might be a water dog* sticking its neck out of the mud," he in-

---

*water dog: spring salamander

sisted. I shook my head, and we went on, the sun in our faces, the road curving beyond sight.

"I've heard they do strange things at the Settlement School at the forks," Dan said, "but I've forgot what they are."

"They have a great bell hung on a pole," I recounted, "and they ring it to get out of bed in the morning and pull on it to memory themselves to eat. Between classes in their schoolhouse they ring a sheep bell." Menifee Thomas had told me a lot. "Menifee says it's crazy the washing and scrubbing and sweeping they do. They fairly peel the floors with brushes every Saturday." And Menifee has spoken of the many books in the school. Stored in my head were titles of the three Sim Brannon's son Commodore had told me about at Houndshell.

"I bet hit's the truth," Dan said.

"Mommy speaks it's unhealthy keeping dust brushed up in the air and forever wetting the boards," said I. "And Menifee claims they've got a jillion cows in a barn. They take soap and a broom and scrub every cow before they milk. Menifee swears they'll next begin brushing the cows' teeth."

"I bet hit's the truth," Dan said.

"But the pranking with the critters doesn't seem to hurt them. They give so much milk everybody has a God's plenty."

The sun-ball tipped the beech trees on the ridge. It grew cooler. We paused again in a horsemint patch, Dan spitting on his big toe, slackening the pain. He said, "I ought not to a-dreamt to go to the Settlement School."

"There never was a pure scholar amongst all of our kin," I reminded. "Not a one who went clear through the books and come out on yon side. I'm of an opinion we ought to do it. And Pap says if we make it, he'll send Holly. And Mittie Hyden's folks might send her." I hadn't forgotten Mittie Hyden. Pap must have known something I hadn't suspected he knew.

"Hit'll take an awful spell of time," Dan said.

We pitied ourselves a mite. We were already missing Sporty Creek. We missed Pap and Mother. And Holly and the baby.

We were about to start again when hooves rattled down the valley, at first distant and faint. We waited, lolling a bit more. Presently a bright-faced nag rounded the creek curve, setting hooves carefully among the wheel tracks. Saul Hignight was in the saddle, riding with feet out of the stirrups, for his legs were too long. He halted beside us, looking down where we squatted, and we saw he recognized us. We arose and shifted our feet.

"Appears your pappy is sending you to the boarding school at the forks for an education," Saul guessed. "Aiming for you to soak up a lot of fool notions."

"Pap never sent us," I said. "We made our own minds." Although we had made up our own minds, Uncle Jolly had stuck the idea there.

Saul lifted his hat and scratched his head. "I don't put much store in these brought-on teachings, burdening the flesh with unnatural things, not a speck of profit to anybody."

"Nothing wrong with learning to cipher, and read, and write," I said.

"I've heard they teach the earth is round," Saul said, "and such a claim goes against Scripture. The Book says plime-blank hit has four corners. Who ever saw a ball with a corner?"

We listened, saying neither yea nor nay. I expected him to mention the calf he had brought to Old Place with a cob in its throat. The calf now was nearly a cow. Yet Saul's mind stayed in the rut of his thinking. He was a Hebron Dunford all over again.

Saul patted his nag and scowled. His voice rose. "There's a powerful mess of tomfoolery taught children nowadays, a-pouring in till they've got no more judgment than a granny-hatchet. Allus I've held a little learning is a blessing, sharpening the mind like a saw blade. Too much knocks the edge off, injures the body's reckoning."

Dan's mouth opened. He wagged his head, agreeing.

"Hain't everybody understand what to swallow and what to cull," Saul warned. "Was I you, young and tender-minded, I'd play hardhead at the school and let only the truth sink past the skull. I believe the Almighty put our brains in a bone box to keep the devilment strained out."

Saul clucked his nag. She started, jerking her long muzzle, straightening her tail. "You young sprouts," he spoke over his shoulder, "don't let 'em put nothing over on you." His mouth kept working, but his words were lost under the clatter of hooves.

"I bet what that fellow says is Gospel," Dan said, staring after the disappearing nag. "I'm scared I can't tell what is fact and what hain't. If'n I was your age, I'd know. I'm afeared I'll swallow a lie-tale."

"Saul Hignight doesn't know square to the end of creation," I said. Again I thought of Little Jolly, of the day he walked his first step. He had risen up, put a foot forward, and toppled. Up he stood again, brave and certain, heading for the door, going from us. Mother had wept, and Pap's eyes got red.

We went on. The sun-ball reddened, flushing the sky. Dan plodded beside me, holding to a corner of the budget, barely lifting his feet above the ruts. His lips were pressed together, his eyes blurred.

"I counted on you getting homesick," I said. But I was homesick as well. My chest felt hollow. I experienced a

yearning I could not name. I knew then that Sporty Creek would forever beckon to me.

Bull bats flew the valley after the sun had set, fluttering sharp wings, slicing the air. A whippoorwill called. Shadows thickened in the laurel patches.

We came upon the forks of Troublesome Creek in early evening and looked down upon the Settlement School from the ridge. Lights were bright in windows, though shapes of buildings were lost against the hills. We rested, listening. No sound came out of the strange place where the lights were, unblinking and cold.

I stood up, hoisting the budget once more. Dan arose slowly, dreading the last steps.

"I ought never thought to be a scholar," Dan said. His voice was small and tight, and the words trembled on his tongue. He caught my hand, and I felt the blunt edge of his palm where the fingers were gone. We started down the ridge, picking our way through stony dark.

THE AUTHOR

James Still is the author of two other popular books from Putnam's, *The Wolfpen Rusties: Appalachian Riddles and Gee-Haw Wimmy-Diddles* and *Way Down Yonder on Troublesome Creek: Appalachian Riddles and Rusties.* Living in rural Knott County, Kentucky, he writes about a people, a land, and a way of life he knows well. Born in Alabama and educated at the University of Illinois and Vanderbilt University, Mr. Still moved into the Kentucky hills in the 1930s. Critics have hailed his verse and fiction for their beauty, humor, and integrity.

THE ARTIST

Janet McCaffery illustrated Mr. Still's two other books for Putnam's with amusing woodcuts which helped make those books popular with a wide reading audience. Ms. McCaffery lives and works in New York City, where she has illustrated many books for young readers. *The Swamp Witch,* which she wrote and illustrated, was chosen by the American Institute of Graphic Arts as one of the best designed children's books of the year.